Walter Besant, James Rice

By Celia's Arbour - A Tale of Portsmouth Town

Vol. II

Walter Besant, James Rice

By Celia's Arbour - A Tale of Portsmouth Town
Vol. II

ISBN/EAN: 9783337079079

Printed in Europe, USA, Canada, Australia, Japan

Cover: Foto ©Andreas Hilbeck / pixelio.de

More available books at **www.hansebooks.com**

A Tale of Portsmouth Town.

[REPRINTED FROM THE "GRAPHIC."]

BY

WALTER BESANT AND JAMES RICE,

AUTHORS OF

"READY-MONEY MORTIBOY," "THE GOLDEN BUTTERFLY," "MY LITTLE GIRL," "WITH HARP AND CROWN," "THIS SON OF VULCAN," "THE CASE OF MR. LUCRAFT," "WHEN THE SHIP COMES HOME," "THE MONKS OF THELEMA," ETC., ETC.

IN THREE VOLUMES.

VOL. II.

LONDON:
SAMPSON LOW, MARSTON, SEARLE, & RIVINGTON,
CROWN BUILDINGS, 188, FLEET STREET, E.C.
1878.

CONTENTS OF VOL. II.

CHAPTER		PAGE
I.	THE RIGHT OF REVOLT	1
II.	THE WORLD AND THE WORD . .	18
III.	A NIGHT UP THE HARBOUR . .	30
IV.	MRS. PONTIFEX ASKS WHAT IT MEANS	61
V.	THE CONSPIRATOR	79
VI.	WASSIELEWSKI'S SECRET . . .	94
VII.	THE MASSACRE OF THE INNOCENTS .	112
VIII.	THE DAY BEFORE . . .	127
IX.	THE TWENTY-FIRST OF JUNE . .	143
X.	A SURPRISE	162
XI.	LEONARD TELLS HIS STORY . .	174
XII.	LEONARD CONTINUES HIS STORY .	191

CHAPTER		PAGE
XIII.	A FRIENDLY CHAT	207
XIV.	A TRIUMPHAL PROCESSION	224
XV.	AN APPEAL TO COMMON SENSE	246
XVI.	A DIPLOMATIST	257
XVII.	THE FOURTH ESTATE	268

BY CELIA'S ARBOUR.

CHAPTER I.

THE RIGHT OF REVOLT.

THE Polish Barrack in 1858 had ceased to exist. There were, in fact, very few Poles left in the town to occupy it. A good many were dead. Some went away in 1854 to join the Turks. Some, grown tired of the quasi-garrison life, left it, and entered into civil occupations in the town. Some, but very few, drifted back to Poland and made their peace with the authorities. Some emigrated. Of all the bearded men I knew as a boy scarcely twenty were left, and these were scattered about the town, still in the "enjoyment" of the tenpence a day granted them by the British Government. I seldom met any of them except Wassielewski, who never wearied of his paternal care. The old man still pursued his calling—that of a fiddler to the sailors. The times, however, were changed. Navy agents were things of the past—a subject of wailing among the Tribes. Sailors' Homes were established; the oiled curls had given way to another and a manlier fashion of short hair. The British sailor was in course of transformation. He no longer made it a rule to spend all his money as fast as he received it; he was sometimes a teetotaler; he was sometimes religious, with views of his own about Election; he sometimes read; and though he generally drank when drink was in the way, he was not often picked up blind drunk in the gutter. The Captain said he supposed men could fight as well if they were always sober as if they were sometimes drunk; and that, always provided there were no sea-lawyers aboard, he saw no reason why a British crew should not be all good-character men, though in his day good character often went with malingering. The trade of fiddling, however was still remunerative, and Wassielewski—Fiddler Ben, as the sailors called him—the steadiest and liveliest fiddler of all, had a large *clientèle.*

At this juncture the staunch old rebel, as I have explained, was in spirits, because he had wind of a new movement. The Poles were to make another effort—he was really five years too early, because the rebellion did not begin till 1863, but that was not his fault; it would be once more the duty of every patriot to rally round the insurrection and strike another blow for Fatherland. Not that he looked for success. No one knew better than this hero of a hundred village fights that the game was hopeless. His policy was one of simple devotion. In every generation an insurrection—perhaps half-a-dozen—was to be got up. Every Pole who was killed fertilised the soil with new memories of cruelty and blood. It was the duty, therefore, of every Pole to get killed if necessary. No Red Irreconcilable ever preached a policy so sanguinary and thorough. Out of the accumulated histories of rebellion was to arise, not in his time, indignation so universal that the whole world would with irrepressible impulse rush to rescue Poland from the triple grasp of the Eagles. To bring about this end but one thing was needed—absolute self-sacrifice.

I knew when he met me, the day after Celia's birthday, and told me that the time was coming, what he meant. I, like himself, was to be a victim to the Holy Cause. I was a hunchback, a man of peace, even a Protestant. That did not matter. I bore an historic name, and I was to give the cause the weight of my name as well as the slender support of my person. And, as I have no desire to pose as a hero, I may at once confess that I felt at first little enthusiasm for the work, and regarded my possible future with feelings of unworthy reluctance.

I suppose that Wassielewski saw this, because he tried to inflame my passion with stories of Russian wrong.

As yet I knew, as I have said, little or nothing about my parentage or the story of my birth. That I should be proud because I was a Pulaski ; that I should be brave because I was a Pulaski ; that I owed myself to Poland, because I was a Pulaski--was all I had learned.

I suppose, unless the old patriot lied—and I do not think he did—that no more revolting story of cruel repression exists than that of the Russian treatment of Poland between the years 1830 and 1835. Wassielewski, with calm face and eyes of fire, used to pour out these horrors to me till my brain reeled. He knew them all ; it was his business to know them, and never to forget them or let others forget them. If he met a Pole he would fall to reviving the old memories of Polish atrocities --if he met a "friend of Poland" he would dilate upon them as if he loved to talk of them.

History is full of the crimes of nations, but there is no crime so great, no wickedness in all the long annals of the world, worse than the story of Russia after that revolution of hapless Poland. We are taught to believe that the wickedness of a single man, in some way, recoils upon his own head. that sooner or later he is punished—*raro antecedentem scelestum*—but what about the wickedness of a country ? Will there fall no retribution upon Russia, upon Prussia, upon Austria ? Have the wheels of justice stopped? Or, in some way which we cannot divine, will the sins of the fathers be visited upon the children for the third and fourth generation? We know not. We see the ungodly flourish like a green bay tree, his eyes swelling out with fatness, and there is no sign or any foreshadowing of the judgment that is to fall upon him. We do not want judgment and revenge. We want only such restitution as is possible; for nothing can give us back the men who have died, the women who have sorrowed, the children who have been carried away. But let us have back our country, our liberty, and our lands.

A dream—an idle dream. Poland is no more. The Poles are become Austrians, Prussians, and, above all, Muscovites.

Wassielewski, a very Accusing Spirit, set himself to fill my mind with stories of tyranny and oppression. The national schools suppressed, a foreign religion imposed, the constitution violated, rebels shot—all these things one expects in the history of conquest. What, however, makes the story of Russian barbarism in Poland unique in the History of Tyranny seems the personal part taken by the Czar and the members of his illustrious family. It was the Czar who ordered, in 1824, twenty-five thousand Poles to be carried to the territory of the Tchernemovski Cossacks. The order was issued, with the usual humanity of St. Petersburg, in the dead of winter, so that most of them perished on the way. It was the Czar who, in 1830, on the occasion of a local outbreak in Sebastopol, ordered with his own hand that the only six prisoners—who had been arrested almost at random—should be shot: that thirty-six more were to be apprehended and knouted: that all the inhabitants without distinction should be expelled the town and sent to the villages of the Crimea: and that the place should be razed to the ground. Every clause except the last was exactly carried into effect. It was the Czar who ordered the library of Warsaw to be transported to St. Petersburg. It was the Czar who formed the humane project of brutalising the Polish peasantry by encouraging the sale of spirits by the Jews. It was the Czar who transported thousands of Polish nobles and soldiers to Siberia. And it was the Czar's brother, the Grand Duke Constantine, whose brutality precipitated the rebellion of 1832.

There were two things which Wassielewski as yet hid from me, because they concerned myself too nearly, and because I think he feared the effect they might have upon me. That, so far, was kind of him. It would have been kinder still had he never told them at all. Even now, nearly twenty years since I learned them I cannot think of them without a passionate beating of the heart; I cannot meet a Russian without instinctive and unconquerable hatred: I cannot name Czar Nicholas without mental execration: and not I only, but every Pole by blood, scattered as we are up and down the face of the world, hopeless of recovering our national liberty, content to become peaceful citizens of France, England, or the States, cannot but look on any disaster that befalls Russia as a welcome instalment of that righteous retribution which will some day, we believe, overtake the country for the sins of the Romanoffs.

In those days, however, I had not yet learned the whole. I knew enough, in a general way, to fill my soul with hatred against the Russian name and sympathy with my own people. I had, as yet received no direct intimation from the old conspirator that he expected me, too, to throw in my lot with him. But I knew it was coming.

I was certainly more English than Polish. I could not speak my father's language. I belonged to the English Church, I was educated in the manners of thought common to Englishmen, insular, perhaps, and narrow; when the greatness of England was spoken of I took that greatness to myself, and was glad. England's victories were mine, England's cause my own, and it was like the loss of half my identity to be reminded that I was not a Briton at all, but a Pole, the son of a long line of Poles, with a duty owed to my country. Like most men, when the path of duty seems confused I was content to wait, to think as much as possible of other things, to put it off, always with the possible future unpleasantly visible, a crowd of peasants armed with scythes and rusty firelocks—I among them—a column of gray coats sweeping us down, old Wassielewski lying dead upon the ground, a solitary prisoner, myself, kneeling with bandaged eyes before an open grave with a dozen guns, at twenty paces, pointing straight at my heart. Nor did I yet feel such devotion to Poland as was sufficient to make the prospect attractive. Also I felt, with some shame, that I could not attain to the exasperation at which Wassielewski habitually kept his nerves.

"I hear," said Herr Räumer one evening, "I hear that your friends in Poland are contemplating another insurrection."

"How do you learn that?" I asked.

"I happened to hear something about it from a foreign correspondent," he replied carelessly. "The Russians, who are not fools, generally know what is going on. Up to a certain point things are allowed to go on. That amuses people. It is only by bad management that conspiracies ever get beyond that point. The Grand Duke Constantine in '31 made enormous mistakes. Well, I had a letter from Berlin to-day, and heard something about it. Here we are at the respectable Bramblers'. Come upstairs and talk for half-an-hour."

"Besides," after he had lit a cigar, got out his bottle of Hock, and was seated in his wooden arm-chair—"Besides, one gets foreign papers, and reads between the lines if one is wise. There is a bundle of Cracow papers on the table. Would you like to read them?"

I was ashamed to confess that I could not read my native tongue.

"That is a pity. One multiplies oneself by learning languages."

"Music has only one language. But how many do you know?"

"A few. Only the European languages. German, Russian, French, English. I believe I speak them all equally well. Polish is almost Russian. He who speaks German easily learns Danish, Swedish, and Dutch. Turkish, I confess, I am only imperfectly acquainted with. It is a difficult language."

"But how did you learn all these languages?"

He smiled superior.

"To begin with," he said, "the Eastern Europeans—you are not yourself a stupid Englishman—have a genius for language. There we do not waste our time in playfields, as these English boys do. So we learn—that is nothing—to talk languages. It is so common that it does not by itself advance a man. It is like reading, a part of education. Among other things you see it is useful in enabling me to read papers in Polish, and to get an inkling how things look in that land of patriots. But you do not want papers, you have your friends here. Of course they keep you informed?"

"I have one or two friends among the few Poles that are left. Wassielewski, my father's devoted servant, is one of them."

"Your father's devoted servant! Really! Devoted? That is touching. I like the devotion of that servant who leaves his master to die, and escapes to enjoy an English pension. One rates that kind of fidelity at a very high value."

The man was nothing unless he could sneer. In that respect he was the incarnation of the age, whose chief characteristic is Heine's "universal sneer." No virtue, no patriotism, no disinterested ambition, no self-denial, no toil for others, nothing but self. A creed which threatens to grow, because it is so simple that every one can understand it. And as the largest trees often grow out of the smallest seeds, one cannot guess what may be the end of it.

"You are right, however," he went on, nursing his crossed leg. "At your age, and with your imperfect education, it is natural that you should be generous. It is pleasant in youth to think that a man can ever be influenced by other than personal considerations. I never did think so. But then my school and yours are different."

"Then what was the patriotism of the Poles?"

"Vanity and self-interest, Ladislas Pulaski. Desire to show off—desire to get something better. Look at the Irish. Look at the Chartists. Who led them? Demagogues fighting for a Cause, because the Cause gives them money and notoriety."

"And no self-denial at all?"

"Plenty. For the satisfaction of vanity. Vanity is the chief motive and power in life. All men are vain; all men are ambitious; but most men in time of danger—and this saves us—are cowards. I am sixty-two years of age. I have seen——" here he hesitated a moment—"I have seen many Revolutions and insurrections, especially in 1848. What is my experience? This. In every conspiracy, where there are three men, one of them is a traitor and a spy. Remember that, should your friends try to drag you into a hopeless business. You will have a spy in your midst. The Secret Service knows all that is done. The other two men are heroes, if you please. That is, they pose. Put them up to open trial, and they speechify ; turn them off to be shot and they fold their arms in an heroic attitude. I believe," he added, with a kind of bitterness, "that they actually enjoy being shot?"

"You have really seen patriots shot?"

"Hundreds," he replied, with a careless wave of his hand. "The sight lost its interest to me, so much alike were the details of each."

"Where was it?"

"In——Paris," he replied. "Of course the papers said as little as could be said about the shootings. I am sure, in fact, now I come to remember, that they did enjoy being shot. The Emperor Nicholas, whose genius lay in suppressing insurrections, knew a much better plan. He had his rebels beaten to death ; at least after a thousand strokes there was not much life left. Now, not even the most sturdy patriot likes to be beaten to death. You cannot pose or make fine speeches while you are walking down a double file of soldiers each with a stick in his hand."

The man's expression was perfectly callous : he talked lightly and without the slightest indication of a feeling that the punishment was diabolical.

"Except the theatrical heroes, therefore, the gentlemen who pose, and would almost as soon be shot as not, provided it is done publicly, every man has his price. You only have to find it out."

"I would as soon believe," I cried, "what you said last week—that every woman has her price, too."

"Of course she has," he replied. "Woman is only imperfect man. Bribe her with dress and jewels; give her what she most wants—Love—Jealousy—Revenge—most likely she is guided by one of those feelings, and to gratify that one she will be traitor, spy, informer, anything.

I suppose I looked what I felt, because he laughed, spoke in softer voice, and touched my arm gently.

"Why do I tell you these things, Ladislas Pulaski? It is to keep you out of conspiracies, and because you will never find them out for yourself. You have to do with the *jeunes élèves*, the *ingénues*, the *naïves*, the innocent. You sit among them like a cherubin in a seraglio of uncorrupted houris. Happy boy!

"Keep that kind of happiness," he went on. "Do

not be persuaded by any Polish exile—your father's servant or anybody else—to give up Arcadia for Civil War and Treachery. I spoke to you from my own experience. Believe me, it is wide. If I had any illusions left, the year of Forty-eight was enough to dispel them all. One remembers the crowd of crack-brained theatrical heroes, eager to pose; the students mad to make a new world: the stupid rustics who thought the Day of no work, double pay, and treble rations was actually come. One thinks of these creatures massacred like sheep, and one gets angry at being asked to admire the leaders who preached the crusade of rebellion."

"You speak only of spies, informers, and demagogues. How about those who fought from conviction?"

"I know nothing about them," he replied, looking me straight in the face. "My knowledge of rebels is chiefly derived from the informers?"

It was a strange thing to say, but I came to understand it later on.

He threw his cigar-ash into the fireplace, and poured out a glass of pale yellow wine which he so much loved.

"Never mind my experience," he said, rising and standing over me, looking gigantic with his six feet two compared with my bent and shrunken form, crouched beneath him in a chair. "I am going to rest and be happy. I shall do no more work in the world. Henceforth I devote myself to Celia. Here is the health of my bride. Hoch!"

CHAPTER II.

THE WORLD AND THE WORD.

"COME to us, Cis, for a day or two," I said. "It will be a little change if it only keeps you out of the way of your persecutor."

It was a custom of old standing for Celia to spend a day or two with the Captain—it did us good in brightening up the dingy old house. When Celia was coming we put flowers on the mantel-shelf, the Captain went round rigging up the curtains with brighter ribbons, and he called it hoisting the bunting. The usual severity of our daily fare was departed from, and the Captain brought out, with his oldest flask, his oldest stories.

"He follows me about," she replied. "I can go nowhere without meeting him. If I go into a shop he is at the door when I come out—it is as if I was already his property."

"But he says nothing — he shows no impatience."

"On Sunday evening I spoke to him. I asked him to give up his pursuit. I appealed to his honour—to his pity."

"He has no pity, Cis."

"To his very love for me, if he really loves me. I told him that it was impossible for me to give my consent. I burst into tears—what a shame to cry before him!—and he only laughed and called me his little April girl. 'Laugh, my little April girl, it rejoices me to see the cloud followed by the sunshine.' Then he asked me to tell him what I wanted him to do and he would do it. 'To tell my father that you have given up your project—to go away and leave me.' He said that he would do anything but give up the project: that his hope was more firmly grounded than ever, and that time would overcome my last objections to making him happy. What kind of love can that be which looks only to a way of making oneself happy?"

That had been my kind of love not very long before.

"I cannot speak to my father, but I see that he is changed. Not in his kindness to me, not that—but he is irritable: he drinks more wine than he should, and he is all the evening in his office now—and sometimes I see his eyes following me—poor papa!

"What is the meaning of it, Laddy? People do not usually promise their daughters to old men when they are eight years of age. Yet this is what he says papa did. Why did he do it? Do you think he lent papa money? You know we were not always so well off as we are now."

"I dare say money has something to do with it," I replied. "It seems to me that money has to do with everything that is disagreeable."

"It has," she said. "Why cannot people do without money altogether? But, if that is all, Aunt Jane and my Uncle Pontifex have plenty of money, and they would help me, I am sure."

"We cannot go to them for help yet. Patience, Cis—patience for a fortnight; we will tell Leonard when he comes home, and perhaps the Captain, too."

"Patience," she echoed. "One tries to be patient, but it is hard. It is not only that I could never love Herr Räumer, Laddy, but the very thought of passing my life with him makes me shake and tremble. I am afraid of him, his manner is smooth but his voice is not, and his eyes are too bright and keen. I have seen him when he did not think it necessary to keep up that appearance of gentleness. I know that he despises women, because I once heard him make a cruel little sneer about us. And he pretends—he pretends to be religious, to please mamma. What sort of life should I have with him? What an end, then, would there be to our talks and hopes!"

I murmured something weak about the higher life being possible under all conditions, but I did not believe it. Life with Herr Räumer—the man who believed religion to be the invention of the priests—that this life was the beginning and the end; that there was nothing to be looked for from man and womankind but from love of self, no honour, no virtue. What could the future of a girl exposed to daily and hourly influences of such a man be like?

Love of self? Would it be, then, for love of self that Celia would accept him?

I suppose for strong natures life might be made to yield the fruits of the most sublime Christianity anywhere, even in a convict hulk; but most of us require more fitting conditions. It is happy to think that no man is tried beyond his strength to bear, although in these latter days we have gone back to the old plan of making new hindrances to the maintenance of the higher spiritual levels, and calling them helps. There are plenty of daily crosses in our way, which call for all our strength, without adding the new and barbaric inconveniences of hunger and small privations. Fasting, as a Ritualist the other day confessed to me, only makes people cross. I should have pitied any girl, even the most commonplace of good English girls, whom Fate might single out to marry this cynical pessimist; how much more when the girl was one whose standard was so high and heart so pure! Should the clear current of a mountain stream be mingled with the turbid water of a river in which no fish can live, foul from contact with many a factory by which it has wound its way, and from which it has brought nothing but the refuse and the scum? Are there not some men—I am sure Herr Räumer was one—who, as they journey through the world, gather up all its wickedness, out of which they construct their own philosophy of existence? And this philosophy it was which he proposed to teach Celia.

"I shall instruct that sweet and unformed mind," he said to me one evening in his lordly way, as if all was quite certain to come off that he proposed, "in the realities of the world. She is at present like a garden full of pretty, delicate flowers—your planting, my young friend; they shall be all pulled up, and we shall have instead—well—those flowers which go to make a woman of the world."

"I do not want to see Celia made into a woman of the world."

"You will not be her husband, Ladislas Pulaski. You only love her like a brother, you know. Ha! ha! And that is very lucky for me. And you do not know what a woman of the world is."

"Tell me what she is."

"I shall not go on living here. I shall live in London, Paris, Vienna, somewhere. My wife shall be a woman who will know from my teaching how to deal with men, and how to find out women. As for the men, she shall play with them like a cat with a mouse. She shall coax their little secrets out of them, especially if they are diplomats; she shall make them tell her what she pleases."

"Why should they not tell her what she pleases? What secrets would Celia wish to hear?"

"*Jeune premier—Cherubin*—you know nothing. They will be political secrets, and my wife will learn them for me. It is only France and Russia which really understand the noble game of feminine intrigue. I shall take my bride away, train her carefully, and with her take my proper place."

Always in the Grand Style; always this talk about diplomacy, secret service and intrigue, and sometimes betraying, or perhaps ostentatiously showing, a curiously intimate acquaintance with Courts and Sovereigns. What, I wondered, was the previous history of this strange man?

"Celia has everything to learn, and a good deal to unlearn," he went on thoughtfully. I do not blame you in any particular, Ladislas. You have done your best. But she has to forget the old-fashioned provincial—or insular—axioms."

"God forbid."

He laughed.

"You forget that you are not an Englishman, but a Slav. They are very pretty—these insular notions—that people marry for love—that people must always answer truthfully, whatever comes of it—that if you want to get a thing you only have to march straight forward—that you must let your friends know all you intend to do—that men care for anything but themselves—that——"

He stopped for want of breath.

"Pray go on," I said; "let us have the whole string of virtues dismissed as insular."

"Marriage for love! Was there ever greater nonsense? The best union that the history of the world speaks of was that of the Sabine maidens carried off by the Romans—carried off by perfect strangers. Picture to yourself the feelings of a proper English young lady under such circumstances. Celia certainly will never love me, but in time, in a short time, you shall see. When a girl sees, that a man is in earnest, that if she appeals to his pity, he laughs; if to his mercy he laughs; if to such trifles as disparity of religion or of age, he laughs—why, you see that woman ends by giving in. Besides it is a compliment to her. I know that I have not your influence or good wishes. I did not expect them, and can do without them. You are as *romanesque* as your pupil—*ça va sans dire.* But I have her father's. She looks very pretty—very sweet indeed—when she gives me one of those upward looks of hers which mean entreaty. What will she be when I have trained her to use those eyes for political purposes?"

It reminded me of a boy with a mouse in a trap. You know how pretty the creature is, her eyes bright with terror and despair, looking at you through the bars which she has been frantically gnawing all the night. Shame and pity to kill the pretty thing. One might tame her. So Herr Raumer, like the schoolboy, admired his prisoner. She was caught in his cage: at least he thought so: she amused him: she pleased his fancy: he would keep her for himself, caged and tamed.

So Celia came to us.

"I am in trouble," she said to the Captain, "and

I came here. Laddy knows what sort of trouble it is, but we ought not to speak of it just yet. Say something, dear Captain, to help us."

The Captain in his simple way took her in his arms and kissed her.

"What trouble can you have that your friends cannot get you out of? I won't ask. There are troubles enough of all sorts. All of them come from somebody disobeying orders. Have you followed instructions, my dear?"

"I have tried to, Captain."

"Then there will be no great harm done, be sure. 'Like a tree planted by the rivers of water, his leaf shall not wither.' Now I tell you what we will do. We will blow some of the trouble away by a sail up the harbour. First let us have tea."

"I remember," the Captain said, when he had finished his tea; "I remember in the action of Navarino, which you may have heard of, my pretty—— Laddy, what are you sniggering at? Of course Celia has heard of Navarino. Very well, then, you shall not hear that story, though it might be brought to bear upon the present trouble.

The best of sea actions is the use they can be put to in all sorts of private affairs. That is not generally known, Celia, my dear: and it makes an action the more interesting to read. Nelson's example always applies. Lay your guns low—nail your colours to the mast—pipe all hands for action: and then—alongside the enemy, however big she is. As to the rest, that's not your concern—and it's in good hands."

"I wish I knew what my duty was," said Celia.

"I wish you did, my dear. And you will know, turning it over in your own mind. I thank God that my life has been a simple one. I never saw any doubt about the line of duty. My orders have always been plain. My children," he added, solemnly, "we all start in life with sealed orders. Some men, when they open them, find them difficult to understand. Now the way to understand them—they are all here"—he laid his hand upon a certain book on the small table beside him—"is to remember, first of all, that duty has got to be done, and that we are not always out on a holiday cruise in pleasant waters."

"I know," said Celia, "I know, Captain"—the tears standing in her eyes.

"They talk about church-going and sermons," the Captain went on, "well—it's part of the discipline. Must have order; church belongs to it—and I'm a plain man, not asked for an opinion. But, Cis, my dear, and Laddy, there's one thing borne in upon me every day stronger. It is that we've got a model always before us. As Christ lived, we must live; those who live most like Him, talk the least, because they think the more. I read once, in a book, of a statue of Christ. Now whoever went to see that statue, however tall he was, found it just a little taller than himself. It was a parable, Celia, I suppose. And it means that the nearer you get to Christ the more you find that you cannot reach Him. Be good, my children. And now, Celia, if you will put on your hat, we will start. It's a fine evening, with a fair breeze, and we need not be back before nine. No more talk about troubles till to-morrow."

CHAPTER III.

A NIGHT UP THE HARBOUR.

THE sun was still high, but fast sloping westwards ; there was a strong breeze blowing up the harbour from the south-west, the tide was full, the water was bright, its wavelets touched by the sunshine, each one sparkling like a diamond with fifty facets, the old ships, bathed in the soft evening light, looked as if they were resting from a long day's work, the hammers in the Dockyard were quiet, and though the beach was crowded it was with an idle throng who congregated together to talk of ships, and they naturally tended in the direction of the beach because the ships were in sight as illustrations. We kept our oars and mast with the running-gear in safety in one of the houses on the

Hard behind a shop. It was a strange and picturesque shop, where everything was sold that was useless and interesting—a museum of a shop; in the window were Malay creases taken in some deadly encounter with pirates in the narrow seas; clubs richly carved and ornamented for some South Sea Island chief; beads worked in every kind of fashion; feathers, bits of costume, everything that a sailor picks up abroad, brings home in his chest, and sells for nothing to such an omnivorous dealer as the owner of this shop. He, indeed, was as strange as his shop. He had been a purser's clerk, and in that capacity had once as strange an experience as I ever heard. He told it me one evening when, by the light of a single candle, I was looking at some things in his back parlour. Some day, perhaps, I will tell you that story. Not now. Some day, too, perhaps, I will write down what I can recollect of the stories he told me connected with his collection. There is no reason now for suppressing them any longer; he is dead, and all those whose mouthpiece he was are dead too. I think that in every man over forty there lies, mostly only known to himself, a strange and wondrous tale.

Could he tell it as it really happened, it would be the story of how events perfectly commonplace in the eyes of other people acted upon him like strokes of Fate, crushing the higher hope that was in him, and condemning him to penal servitude for life, to remain upon the lower levels. Because it is mostly true that many run, but to one only is given the prize. Am I—are you—the only one whom fortune has mocked? *Nos numerus sumus*, the name of the Unfortunate is Legion; no one has the exclusive right to complain. To fifty Fate holds out the golden apples of success, and one only gets them.

We took our sculls and sails from the shop, and rigged our craft. She was built something on the lines of a wherry, for seaworthiness, a strong, serviceable boat, not too heavy for a pair of sculls, and not too light to sail under good press of canvas. Everybody knew us on the beach—the boatmen, the old sailors, and the sailors' wives who were out with the children because the weather was so fine, all had a word to say to the Captain, touching their forelocks by way of preface. One carried our oars, another launched the boat, another sent a boy for a couple of rough sea-rugs, because the wind was high, and the young lady might get wet, and in the midst of the general excitement we jumped in and pushed off.

Celia sat in the stern, one of the rugs serving as a cushion, and held the rudder-strings. The Captain sat opposite her, I took the sculls to row her clear of the beach, until we could hoist our sail.

"This is what I like," said the Captain, dragging a little more of the waterproof over Celia's feet in his careful way. "A bright day, a breeze aft, but not dead aft—Laddy, we shall have some trouble getting back—a tight little boat, and a pretty girl like little Cis in command. Aha! Catch an old salt insensible to lovely woman.

"'Blow high, blow low, let tempests tear
The mainmast by the board;
My heart with thoughts of thee, my dear.
And love well stored.'"

Celia laughed. Her spirits rose as each dip of the sculls lengthened our distance from the shore, and made her certain of escaping, at least for one evening, from her persecutor. She wore some pretty sort of brown holland stuff made into a jacket, and braided with a zig-zag Vandyke pattern in red. I do not know how I remember that pattern of the braid, but it seems as if I remember every detail of that evening—her bright and animated face flushed with the pleasure and excitement of the little voyage, rosy in the evening sunshine, the merry eyes with which she turned to greet the Captain's little compliment, the halo of youth and grace which lay about her, the very contour of her figure as she leaned aside, holding both the rudder-strings on one side. I remember the little picture just as if it was yesterday.

Outside the ruck of boats which came and went between the opposite shores of the port we were in free and open water, and could ship the sculls and hoist our sail for a run up the harbour.

The sail up, I came aft, and sat down in the bottom of the ship, while the Captain held the rope and Celia the strings. And for a space none of us talked.

Our course carried us past the Docks and the shore-line buildings of the Dockyard. There were the white wharves, the cranes, the derricks, and all sorts of capstans, chains, and other gear for lifting and hoisting ; the steam-tugs were lying alongside ; all as deserted and as quiet as if the Yard belonged to some old civilisation. Bright as the evening was, the effect was rather ghostly, as we glided, silent save for the rippling at the bows, along the silent bank. Presently, we came to the building-sheds. Some of them were open and empty ; some were closed ; within each of the closed sheds lay, we knew, the skeleton, the half-finished frame, of a mighty man-o'-war—some of them but just begun ; some ready to be launched ; some, the deserted and neglected offspring of some bygone First Lord's experimental ignorance, lying as they had lain for thirty years, waiting for the order to be finished off and launched.

"Think of the twilight solitude in those great empty sheds, Cis," I whispered. "Think of the ghosts of wrecked ships haunting the places where they were built when the moonlight streams in at the windows. Fancy seeing the transparent outline of some old three-decker, say the great *Victory*, as she went down with a thousand men aboard, lying upon the timber-shores——"

"With the ghosts of the old shipbuilders," said

Celia, "walking about with their hands behind them, criticising the new-fashioned models."

"More likely to be swearing at steam," said the Captain. The new-fashioned models! Where are they now, the ships which were on the slips twenty years ago? The *Duke of Marlborough*, the *Prince of Wales*, the *Royal Frederick*, the *Royal Sovereign*—Where is last year's snow? They are harbour ships, ships cut down and altered into ironclads, and of a date gone out of fashion."

There were many more ships in harbour then than now; we had not yet learned to put all our trust in iron, and where we have one serviceable fighting vessel now we had twenty then. No hulk in the good old days, that could float and could steer but could fight; there were no torpedoes, no rams, no iron vessels, no venomous little monitors. To lay yourself alongside an enemy and give broadside for broadside till one tired of it, was the good old fashion of a naval battle. What is it now?

Again, twenty years ago, they did not break up and destroy every vessel that seemed to be past service. She was towed up harbour and left there moored in her place, to furnish at least house accommodation for a warrant officer, if she could be of no other use. There were hundreds of ships there lying idle, their work over; some of them were coal hulks, some convict hulks, some receiving hulks; most were old pensioners who did no work any more, floating at high tide, and at low lying in the soft cushion of the harbour mud. Presently we ran among them all, passing in and out, and through their lines. Then I took the rudder-strings, so that Celia might look while the Captain talked.

He pushed his hat well back, sat upright, and began to look up and down the familiar craft with the eye of an old friend anxious to see them looking their best. It was not much they could show in the way of decoration, but the figure-heads were there still, and the balconies and carvings of the stern, were mostly uninjured. As for the hull, it had generally been painted either black, white, or yellow. There were no masts, but they had jury-masts to serve as derricks on occasion. "That is the *Queen Charlotte*, my dear. She was flagship at Algiers when Lord Exmouth showed the Moors we would stand no more nonsense. We've fought a good many naval actions, but I think that business was about the best day's work we ever did. I was chasing Arab dhows and slavers off Zanzibar, and hadn't the chance of doing my share of the work. In 1816, that was——

"Look—look—Celia! Look, children. There's the old *Asia*. God bless her! Flagship, Celia, at Navarino. My old ship—my one battle. Ah! Navarino. They say now it was a mistake, and that we only played the Russians' game. No chance of doing that again. But anyhow it was a glorious victory." The recollection of that day was always too much for the Captain, and he might have gone on the whole evening with personal reminiscences of the battle, but for the breeze which freshened up and carried us past the *Asia*.

"No confounded steam," he growled, "no wheels and smoke spoiling the decks; quiet easy sailing, and no noise allowed aboard until the guns began to speak. Port, Laddy. That is the *Princess Charlotte*, Celia. Forty people were drowned when she was launched; and a good many more went below when she made herself heard at Acre. I was not there either, more's the pity. I was cruising about the narrow seas picking up pirates off Borneo.

"There is the *Egmont.* She fought the French fleet in 1795, and the Spaniards in 1797. Good old craft. Stout old man-o'-war.

"That is the *Illustrious*, moored in line with the *Egmont.* She was with her in '95, and I think she helped to take Java in 1811. We used, in those days, you see, Celia, if we wanted a place that belonged to the enemy, just to go and take it. Not that we were so unmannerly as not to give them a civil choice. We used to say, Gentlemen, Señors Caballeros, Mynheer Double Dutchmen,' as the case might be, 'we've come here to haul down your bunting and run up the Union Jack over your snug quarters. So, as perhaps you would not like to give in without a bit of a fight, you had better ram in your charge, and we'll give you a lead.' Then the action began, and after a respectable quantity of powder was burned they struck their colours, we went ashore, the men had a spree, and the officers made themselves agreeable to the young ladies."

"Did not the young ladies object to making friends with the enemy?"

"Not at all, my dear. Why should they? We did them no wrong, and we generally represented the popular side; they wanted to be taken by the British Fleet, which meant safety as well as flirtation. And we enjoyed our bit of fighting first. Did you ever hear of Captain Willoughby in Mahébourg Bay, Island of Mauritius? Well, that's an unlucky story, because it ended badly, and instead of Willoughby taking the island the island took him. Ran his ship ashore. She turned on her side, so that her guns couldn't be brought to bear. They found the captain with one eye out and a leg shot off. The French captain had a leg shot off too, and so they put them both in the same bed, where they got better, and drank each other's health. The worst of it was that what we sailors got for England the politicians gave away again when they signed a peace. We let the Dutch have Java, we let the French have Bourbon and Guadaloupe. I wonder we didn't give New Zealand to the Americans, and I dare say we should if they had thought of asking for it.

"That is the *Colossus*, my dear. Good old ship, too; she was at Trafalgar. There is the *Alfred*, who helped to take Guadaloupe in 1810, and the *Æolus* frigate. She fired a shot or two at

Martinique the year before. Look at them, the row of beauties; forty-two pounders, the handiest and most murderous craft that ever went to sea; and look at the sloops and the little three-gun brigantines. I had one under my command once. And there is the *Columbine.*"

The Captain began to sing:

"'The *Trinculo* may do her best,
And the *Alert* so fleet, Sir,
Alert she is, but then she's not
Alert enough to beat, Sir.

. . . .

The *Acorn* and the *Satellite*,
Their efforts, too, may try, Sir,
But if they beat the *Columbine*,
Why, dash it!—they must fly, Sir.'

"They will build no more such ships; seamanship means poking the fire. Look at those things now."

He pointed with great contempt to the war steamers. Those of 1858 would be thought harmless things enough now. Two or three had screws, but most had the old paddles. The *Duke of Wellington* of 130 guns carried a screw; so did the *Blenheim*, the *Archer*, and the *Encounter*, all of which were lying in the harbour. But the *Odin*, the *Basilisk*, and the *Sidon* were splendid paddle steamers. Among them lay the *Megæra*, a troop ship, afterwards wrecked on St. Paul's Island; the Queen's steam yacht, the *Fairy*, as pretty a craft as ever floated, in which Her Majesty used to run to and fro between Osborne and the port; the *Victoria and Albert*, the larger Royal yacht; and the pretty little *Bee*, smallest steamer afloat, before they invented the noisy little steam launches to kill the fish, to tear down the banks of the rivers, and to take the bread out of the mouths of the old wherrymen in our harbour.

We were drawing near the last of the big ships.

"There, Celia, look at that craft," cried the Captain. "Do you see anything remarkable about her?"

"No; only she is yellow."

"That is because she is a receiving hulk," he informed her, with the calmness that comes of a whole reservoir of knowledge behind. "It is in her cut that I mean. Don't you remark the cut of her stern, the lines of her bows?"

She shook her head, and laughed.

"Oh! the ignorance of womankind," said the Captain. "My dear, she's French. Now you see?"

Again Celia shook her head.

"Well," he sighed, "I suppose it's no use trying to make a young lady understand such a simple thing. If it had been a bit of lace now, or any other fal-lal and flap-doodle—never mind, my pretty, you're wise enough upon your own lines. That is the *Blonde*, my dear, and she is one of the very last of the old prizes left. When she is broken up I don't know where I could go to look for another of the old French prizes. My father, who was a Master in the Navy, navigated her into this very port. She struck her flag off Brest.

"It is a page of history, children," he went on, "this old harbour. They ought to keep all the ships just as they are, and never break up one till she drops to pieces. The brave old ships! It seems a shame, too, to turn them into coal hulks and convict hulks. I would paint them every year, and keep them for the boys and girls to see.

'These are the craft of the old fighting bulldogs,' I would tell them. 'You've got to fight your own battles in a different sort of way. But be bulldogs, however you go into action, and you'll pull through just as your fathers did.'

"I saw a sight when I was a boy," the Captain went on, "that you'll never see again, unless the Lords of the Admiralty take my advice and give over breaking-up ships. I saw the last of the oldest ship in the service. She was the *Royal William*, eighty guns. That ship was built for Charles the Second, sailed for James the Second, and fought off and on for a hundred and forty years. Then they broke her up—in 1812—because, I suppose, they were tired of looking at her. She ought to be afloat now, for sounder timber you never saw."

"Shall we down sail and out sculls?" I asked.

The Captain answered by a gesture, and we kept on our course. The tide was running out rapidly.

"Five minutes more, Laddy," he said. "We've time to go as far as Jack the Painter's Point, and then we'll come down easy and comfortable with the last of the ebb."

We had left the lines of ships and hulks behind us now, and were sailing over the broad surface of the upper harbour, where it is wise even at high tide to keep to the creeks, the lines of which are indicated by posts. In these there lay, so old that they had long since been forgotten, some half-a-dozen black hulls, each tenanted by a single ex-warrant officer with his family. Even the Captain, who knew most ships, could not tell the history of these mysterious vessels. What life, I used to think as a boy, could compare with that of being the only man on board one of these old ships? Fancy being left in charge of such a vessel, yourself all alone, or perhaps with Leonard moored alongside, also in charge of one. Robinson Crusoe in his most solitary moments could not have felt happier. Then to wander and explore the great empty ship; to open the cabin and look in the old lockers; to roam about in the dim silences of the lower deck, the twilight of the orlop; the mysterious shades of the cockpit, and to gaze down the impenetrable Erebus of the hold.

To this day I can never go on board a great ship without a feeling of mysterious treasures and strange secrets lurking in the depths below me. And what a place for ghosts! think, if you could constrain the ghosts on those old ships to speak, what tales they could tell of privateering, of pirating, of perils on the Spanish Main, of adventure, of pillage, and of glory. There may be a ghost or two in old inns, deserted houses, ruined castles, and country churchyards. But they are nothing, they can be nothing, compared with the ghosts on an old ship lying forgotten up the harbour. Cis shudders, and thinks she can get on very well without ghosts, and that when she wants their society she would rather meet them ashore.

"That ships may be haunted," said the Captain, gravely, "is true beyond a doubt. Every sailor will tell you that. Did you never hear how we were haunted aboard the *Fearnought* by the ghost of the purser's clerk?"

I have always regretted, for Celia's sake, that we did not hear that story. The Captain stopped because we were close on Jack the Painter's Point, and we had to attend to the boat.

The Point was a low-lying narrow tongue of land, with one solitary tree upon it, running out into the harbour. It had an edging or beach of dingy sand, behind which the turf began, in knots of long coarse grass, between which, at high tide, the ground was soft and marshy; when the water was out it was difficult to tell where the mud ended and the land began. Now, when the tide was at its highest, the little point, lapped by the waves, and backed by its single tree, made a pretty picture. It was a lonely and deserted spot, far away from any house or inhabited place; there was not even a road near it; behind was a barren field of poor grass where geese picked up a living with anxiety and continual effort; and it was haunted by the gloomiest associations, because here the ghost of Jack the Painter walked.

It was not a fact open to doubt, like some stories of haunted places; Jack had been seen by a crowd of witnesses, respectable mariners, whose testimony was free from any tinge of doubt. It walked after nightfall: It walked backwards and forwards, up and down the narrow tongue of land: It walked with Its hands clasped behind Its neck, and Its head bent forward as if in pain. Anybody might be in pain after hanging for years in chains.

Imitate that action, and conjure up, if you can, the horror of such an attitude when assumed by a ghost.

The story of Painter Jack was an episode in the last century. He belonged to the fraternity of ropemakers, a special Guild in this port, the members of which enjoyed the privilege, whenever the Sovereign paid the place a visit, of marching in procession, clad in white jackets, nankeen trousers, and blue sashes, in front of the Royal carriage. The possession of his share in this privilege ought to have made Jack, as it doubtless made the rest of his brethren, virtuous and happy. It did not: Jack became moody, and nursed thoughts of greatness. unfortunately, his ambitions led him in the same direction as those of the illustrious Eratostratus. He achieved greatness by setting fire to the rope-walk. They found out who had done it, after the fire was over and a vast amount of damage had been done, and they tried the unlucky Jack for the offence. He confessed, made an edifying end, and was hanged in chains on that very point which now bears his name. It was in 1776, and twenty years ago there were still people who remembered the horrid gibbet and the black body, tarred, shapeless, hanging in chains, and swinging stridently to and fro in the breeze. Other gentlemen who were gibbeted in the course of the same century had friends to come secretly and take them down. Mr. Bryan, for instance, was one. He for a brief space kept company with Painter Jack, hanging beside him, clad handsomely in black velvet, new shoes, and a laced shirt. He was secretly removed by his relations. Williams the Marine was another; he was popular in the force, and his comrades took him down. So that poor Jack was left quite alone in that dreary place, and partly out of habit, partly because it had no more pleasant places of resort, the ghost continued to roam about the spot where the body had hung so long.

"Down sail, out sculls," said the Captain. "Hard a port, Celia. We'll drop down easy and comfortable with the tide. How fast it runs out!"

It was too late to think of tacking home with the wind dead against us, and the tide was strong in our favour. I took the sculls and began mechanically to row, looking at Celia. She was more silent now. Perhaps she was thinking of her persistent lover, for the lines of her mouth were set hard. I do not know what the Captain was thinking of; perhaps of Leonard. However that may be, we were a boat's crew without a coxswain for a few minutes.

"Laddy!" cried the Captain, starting up, "where have we got to?"

I held up and looked round. The tide was running out faster than I had ever known it. We were in the middle of one of the great banks of mud, and there was, I felt at once, but a single inch betwen the keel and the mud. I grasped the sculls again, and pulled as hard as I knew; but it was of no use. The next moment we touched; then a desperate struggle to pull her through the mud; then we stuck fast, and, like the water flowing out of a cup, the tide ran away from the mud-bank, leaving us high and dry, fast prisoners for six hours.

We looked at each other in dismay.

Then the Captain laughed.

"Not the first boat's crew that has had to pass

the night on the mud," he said cheerfully. "Lucky we've got the wraps. Celia, my dear, do you think you shall mind it very much? We will put you to sleep in the stern while Laddy and I keep watch and watch. No supper, though. Poor little maid! Poor Celia!"

She only laughed. She liked the adventure.

There was no help for it, not the slightest. Like it or not, we had to pass the night where we were unless we could wade, waist deep, for a mile through black mud to Jack the Painter's Point.

The tide which had left us on the bank had retreated from the whole upper part of the harbour. But the surface of the mud was still wet, and the splendour of the setting sun made it look like a vast expanse of molten gold. One might have been on the broad ocean, with nothing to break the boundless view but a single solitary islet with a tree on it, for so seemed the Point of Painter Jack. The sky was cloudless, save in the west, where the light mists of evening were gathered together, like the courtiers at the *coucher du roi,* to take farewell of the sun, clad in their gorgeous dresses of pearl-grey, yellow, crimson, and emerald.

Athwart the face of the setting sun, a purple cleft in light and cloud, stood up the solitary poplar on the Point. Bathed and surrounded by the western glory, it seemed to have lost all restraints of distance, and to form, in the far-off splendour, part and parcel of the sapphire-tinted west.

As we looked, the sun sank with a plunge, the evening gun from the Duke of York's bastion over the mouth of the harbour saluted the departure of day. The courtier clouds did not immediately disperse, but slowly began putting off their bright apparel.

In a quarter of an hour the outside clouds were grey; in half an hour all were grey; and presently we began to see the stars clear and bright in the cloudless sky.

"The day is gone," murmured Celia, "morn is breaking somewhere beyond the Atlantic. We ought not to let the thoughts of our own selfish cares spoil the evening, but when the sun sank, my heart sank too."

"Faith and Hope, my pretty," said the Captain. "Come, it is nearly nine o'clock. Let us have evening prayers and turn in."

This was our godly custom before supper. The Captain read a chapter— he was not particular what —regarding all chapters as so many Articles or Rules of the ship, containing well-defined duties, on the proper performance of which rested the hope of future promotion. On this occasion we had no chapter, naturally. But we all stood up while the Captain took off his hat and recited one or two prayers. Then Celia and I sang the Evening Hymn. Our voices sounded strange in the immensity of the heavens above us—strange and small.

And then we sat down, and the Captain began to wrap Celia round in the waterproofs. She refused to have more than one, and we finally persuaded him to take one for himself—they were good-sized serviceable things, fortunately—and to leave us the other. We all three sat down in the stern of the boat, the Captain on the boards with his elbow on the seat, and Celia and I, side by side, the rug wrapped round us, close together.

Ashore the bells of the old church were playing their hymn tune, followed by the curfew.

"The bells sound sweetly across the water,"

murmured Celia. "Listen, Laddy, what do they say?"

"I know what the big bell says," I reply. "It has written upon it what it says:

"'We good people all
To prayers do call.
We honour to king,
And brides joy do bring.
Good tidings we tell,
And ring the dead's knell.'"

"'Good tidings we tell,'" she whispers. "What good tidings for us, Laddy?"

"I will tell you presently," I say, "when I have made them out."

The bells cease, and silence falls upon us. It has grown darker, but there is no real darkness during this summer night, only a twilight which makes the shadows black. As we look down the harbour, where the ships lie, it is a scene of enchantment. For the men-o'-war's lights, not regular, but scattered here and there over the dark waters, light up the harbour, and produce an effect stranger than any theatrical scene.

Said the Captain, thinking still of the ships:

"A ship's life is like a man's life. She is put in commission after years of work to fit her up—that's our education. She sails away on the business of the country, she has storms and calms, so have the landlubbers ashore; she has good captains and bad captains; she has times of good behaviour and times of bad; sometimes she's wrecked;—well, there's many a good fellow thrown away so; sometimes she goes down in action, nothing finer than that—and sometimes she spends the rest of her life up in harbour. Well for her if she isn't made a convict hulk. Celia, my dear, you are comfortable, and not too cold?"

"Not a bit cold, Captain, thank you, only rather hungry."

There was no help for that, and the Captain, announcing his intention to turn in, enjoined me to wake him at twelve, so that we two could keep watch and watch about, covered his head with the rug, and in five minutes was fast asleep.

Then Celia and I had the night all to ourselves.

We were sitting close together, with the waterproof round our shoulders. Presently, getting a little cramped, Celia slipped down from the seat, and curled herself up close to the sleeping Captain, resting her head upon my knees, while I laid my arm round her neck.

Was it treachery when I had striven to beat down and conquer a passion which was not by any means fraternal for me to feel as if there had never been a perfect night since the world for me began till this one? I wished it would last for ever. When before had I had my queen all to myself in the long, sweet silences of a summer night? And none to hear what we said.

There was no word of love, because that was all one side, but there was talk. We did not sleep that night. The air was soft and warm, though sometimes came a cold touch of wind which made us pull the wraps tighter, and nestle close to each other. But we talked in low whispers, partly because the night is a sacred time, and partly because we were careful not to wake the Captain.

"Tell me now," she whispered, "tell me the good tidings of the bells."

I thought of Leonard's last secret which he told me when he left me on the platform of the station.

"Tell Cis?" he said; "that would spoil all." Yet I did tell Cis. I told her that night.

"The bells said, Cis, that there only wanted a fortnight to Leonard's return. He will come back brave and strong."

"And he will make all right," she cried, eagerly, clasping my hand in hers. "Go on, Laddy dear."

"He will make all right. The German shall be sent about his business, and—and——"

"And we all shall go on just as we used to, Laddy."

"N—not quite, Cis. When Leonard went away, he told me a great secret. I was not to tell anybody. And I should not tell you now, only that I think it will do good to both of us, that you should know it. Tell me, my sister, you have not forgotten Leonard?"

"Forgotten Leonard? Laddy, how could I?"

"You think of him still. You remember how brave and true he was; how he loved—us both——"

"I remember all, Laddy."

"When he left me, Cis—he told me—Hush! let me whisper—low—low—in your ear—that his greatest hope was to come back in five years' time, a gentleman—to find you free—and to ask you—to ask you, Cis—to marry him."

She did not answer, but as she lay in the boat, her hands holding mine, her face bent down, I felt a tear fall on my finger; I do not think it was a tear of sorrow.

"You are not offended, Cis dear," I whispered; "I have not done wrong in telling you."

"Let it be a secret between you and me, Laddy," she said, presently. "Do not let us ever speak of it again."

"Cis, you told me once that you would hide nothing from me. Tell me—if Leonard asked you——"

She threw her arms round my neck, and hid her face upon my shoulder. "Laddy," she whispered, "there is no day, in all these five years, that I have not prayed, night and morning, for Leonard."

Then we were silent.

The hours sped too swiftly, marked by the bells of the ships in commission. About two in the morning, the tide began to turn, and the day began to break. First, the dull black surface of flats became wet and glittered in the light. Then the water slowly crept up and covered all; it took time to reach us, because we were on a bank. And all the time we watched, the grey in the east grew tinged with all colours; and the wild-fowl rose out of their sleeping-places by the shore, and flew screaming heavenwards in long lines or arrow-headed angles. And presently the sun arose, splendid.

"Laddy," whispered Celia, for the Captain still slept, "this is more glorious than the evening."

At six bells, which is three in the morning, we floated. I noiselessly stepped over the sleeping form of the Captain and took the sculls, dipping them in the water as softly as I could. He did not awake until half an hour later, when our bows struck the beach, and at the noise the Captain started up. It was nearly four o'clock; no boats were on the harbour; the stillness contrasted strangely with the light of the summer morning.

"Laddy," grumbled the Captain, "you've kept double watch. You call that sailor-like?—Celia, my dear, you have not caught cold?"

When we reached home, the Captain insisted on our going to bed.

"We have passed a night I shall never forget, Laddy," said Celia at her door.

"A sacred night, Cis."

She stooped down, my tall and gracious lady, and kissed my forehead.

"What should I do without you, Laddy? To have some one in the world to whom you can tell everything and not be ashamed, not be afraid. To-night has brought us very close together."

I think it had. After it we were more as we had been when children. My Celia, the maiden of sweet reserve, came back to me a child again, and told me all.

No need now to speak again of Leonard. It remained only to look forward and hope and long for the weary days to pass away.

CHAPTER V.

MRS. PONTIFEX ASKS WHAT IT MEANS.

THAT was a night consecrated to every kind of sweet memories. It was quite in the nature of things that it should be followed by one of a more worldly kind. In fact, the next day, to put the matter in plain English, we had a great row, a family row.

It began with Aunt Jane. She came to tea, accompanied by her husband; and she came with the evident intention of speaking her mind. This made us uneasy from the beginning, and although Mrs. Tyrrell attempted to pour oil on the troubled waters by producing her very best tea service, an honour which Mrs. Pontifex was certain to appreciate, she failed. Even tea services in pink and gold, with the rich silver teapot, accompanied by a lavish expenditure in seedcake, and Sally Lunns, and muffins, failed to bring a smile to that severe visage. Mrs. Pontifex was dressed for the occasion in a pyramidal cap trimmed with lace, beneath which her horizontal curls showed like the modest violet peeping between April leaves of grass. She wore her most rustling of black silk robes, and the most glittering of her stud-clasps in the black velvet ribbon which girt her brow. She sat bolt upright in her chair; and such was her remarkable strength of character, testimony to which has already been given by her husband, that she struck the key-note to the banquet, and made it joyless.

Who could be festive when Mrs. Pontifex icily refused sugar with her tea, and proceeded to deny that luxury to her husband?

"No, John Pontifex," she said. "It is high time to set less store upon creature comforts. No sugar, Celia, in my husband's tea."

Mr. Pontifex meekly acquiesced. He was already in the most profound depths of depression when he arrived, and a cup of tea without sugar was only another addition to his burden of melancholy. I conjectured that he had passed the afternoon in the receipt of spiritual nagging. In this art his wife was a proficient; and although nagging of all kinds must be intolerable, I think the religious kind must be the most intolerable. The unfortunate man made no effort to recover his cheerfulness, and sat silent, as upright as his wife, the cup of unsweetened tea in his hand, staring straight before him. Once, his wife looking the other way, he caught my eye and shook his head solemnly.

Under these circumstances we all ran before the gale close reefed.

It was a bad sign that Mrs. Pontifex did not talk. If she had been critically snappish, if she had told her niece that her cap was unbecoming, or Celia that her frock was unmaidenly, or me that an account would be required of me for my idle time—a very common way she had of making things pleasant—one would not have minded. But she did not speak at all, and that terrified us. Now and then she opened her lips, which moved silently, and then closed with a snap, as if she had just framed and fired off a thunderbolt of speech. Her husband remarked one of these movements, and immediately replacing his cup upon the table, softly rose and effaced himself behind the window curtains, where he sat with only a pair of trembling knees visible. Mr. Tyrrell pretended to be at his ease, but was not. His wife was not, and did not pretend to be.

As soon as we reasonably could we rang the bell for the tea-things to be removed, and began some music. This was part of the regular programme, though no one suspected Mrs. Pontifex or her husband of any love for harmony. And while we were playing came Herr Räumer, at sight of whom Mrs. Pontifex drew herself up more stiffly than before, and coughed ominously.

He looked very fresh and young, this elderly foreigner. He was dressed neatly in a buttoned frock (no one in our circle wore evening dress for a gathering under the rank of dinner-party or dance), and had a rose in a button-hole. A little bit of scarlet ribbon in his breast showed that he was the possessor of some foreign Order. In his greeting of Celia he showed a Romeo-like elasticity and youthfulness, and he planted himself on the hearthrug with an assured air, as if the place and all that was in it belonged to him.

In front of him, upon a small couch, sat Mrs. Pontifex, her lips moving rapidly, and her brow darker than ever. Either Herr Räumer was going to interrupt the battle, or he was himself the cause of it. Celia rose from the piano, and sat beside her great-aunt. Mr. Tyrrell was in an easy-chair on one side the fireplace, and his wife on the other, fanning herself, though it was by no means a warm night. As I said before, Mr. Pontifex was in hiding. I sat on the music-stool and looked on. Had there been any way of escape I should have taken advantage of that way. But there was none.

The awful silence was broken by Aunt Jane.

"'Be ye not yoked unequally with unbelievers,'" she said. Then her lips closed with a snap.

No one answered for a while. The curtain alone, behind which was her husband, showed signs of agitation.

"John Pontifex," said his wife. "Assist me."

He obeyed immediately, and took up a position behind her, standing opposite to the German. He looked very, very meek.

"John Pontifex and I were talking this afternoon, Clara Tyrrell and George Tyrrell, and we naturally discussed the strange—the very strange—rumours that are afloat with regard to Celia. Her name, George Tyrrell, has been coupled with that of this—this foreign gentleman here."

Mr. Pontifex shook his head as if more in sorrow than in anger.

"It is—alas!—the fact that such rumours are prevalent."

"You hear, George Tyrrell?" she went on.

"I hear," he replied. "The rumours are not without foundation."

Poor Celia!

"I announced to John Pontifex, this afternoon, my intention of speaking my mind on this matter, and speaking it in the actual presence of Herr Räumer himself, if necessary."

"I am infinitely obliged to you, madam," said that gentleman, with a bow. "I wish that I was already in a position to ask for your congratulations."

"Flap-doodle and fudge," said Aunt Jane. I do not defend this expression, but it was her own, reserved for use on those occasions which required the greatest strength of the English language.

All trembled except the German. Celia, by the way, except that she looked pale, took no apparent interest in the conversation.

"Congratulations are useless ornaments of conversation," he said. "That, I presume, is what you mean, Mrs. Pontifex?"

She snorted.

"Pray, sir,—will you tell us first, to what religious persuasion you belong?"

The unexpected question staggered him for a moment. I thought he was lost. But he recovered.

"My excellent parents," he said, "who are now no longer living, brought me up in the strictest school—Mrs. Pontifex is, I believe, a member of the Anglican Church—of German Calvinism."

"And what church do you attend in this town?"

"Unfortunately, there is no church of my views in this town. The English churches, however, approach my distinctive doctrines near enough for me." He said this meekly, as if conscious of a superiority which he would not press.

"No blessing shall come from me on any marriage

where both members are not communicants of the English Establishment."

She said that with an air of determination, as if the matter was settled.

Herr Räumer laughed softly.

"If that is your only objection, my dear madam, it is easily removed. *Mademoiselle vaut bien une messe.*"

"I do not understand French."

"I mean that love, coupled with a short conversation with your learned husband over a few doctrinal difficulties, would permit me to present myself to you in the novel character of a communicant."

He overacted the speech, and no one could fail to see the sneer behind it.

"John Pontifex."

"My dear, I am—in point of fact—behind you."

"You hear what this gentleman says. You can hold a discussion with him in my presence. If, in my opinion, he proves himself worthy of our Communion I shall withdraw that part of my objection."

"It is true," said John Pontifex, "that I am not at the present moment—alas!—deeply versed in the points which—ahem—separate us from German Calvinism. But no doubt Herr Räumer will enlighten me."

"Or," said the suitor, rolling his head, "let me refer myself to a fairer theologian. Celia herself shall convert me."

Celia made no sign.

"This is mockery," Mrs. Pontifex ejaculated. "But it is what I expected, and indeed said to John Pontifex as we drove here. That a foreigner should value Christian privileges is hardly to be looked for."

"That is, I believe," said Herr Räumer, with the faintest possible suspicion of contempt in his smooth tones, "the prevalent belief among English people. And yet no Englishman has yet publicly doubted that even a foreigner has a soul to be saved."

"Or lost," said Mrs. Pontifex sternly.

Her husband, who was still standing meekly beside her, his long arms dangling at either side, looking exactly like a tall schoolboy afraid of his schoolmaster, groaned audibly.

"Or lost," echoed Herr Räumer.

"And pray, sir, if I may ask, what are your

means of existence? No doubt Mr. Tyrrell knows all about your family and the way in which you get your living, but we have not yet been informed, and we also have an interest in Celia Tyrrell."

"I have private property," he replied, looking at Mr. Tyrrell, "on the nature of which I have satisfied the young lady's father."

"Perfectly, perfectly," said Mr. Tyrrell.

"How do we know but what you have a wife somewhere else—in Germany, or wherever you come from?"

"Madame's intentions are no doubt praiseworthy, though her questions are not perhaps quite conventional. However, there is no question I would not answer to secure the friendship of Celia's great-aunt. I have no wife in Germany. Consider, Mrs. Pontifex, I have resided in this town for some twelve years. Would my wife, if I had one, be contented to languish in solitude and neglect? Would you, Mrs. Pontifex, allow your husband to live as a bachelor—perhaps a wild and gay bachelor—at a distance from yourself?"

The Rev. Mr. Pontifex smiled and sighed. Did he allowed his imagination even for a moment to dwell on the possibility of a wild and rollicking life away from his wife?

"My wild oats," he said, very slowly, with emphasis on each word, and shaking his head. "My—wild—oats—are long since—ahem!—if I may be allowed the figure of speech—sown."

"John Pontifex," said his wife, "we are not interested in your early sins."

"I was about to remark, my dear, that they have produced—alas!—their usual crop of repentance—that is all. The wages of youthful levity——"

"We will allow Herr Räumer," Mrs. Pontifex interrupted her husband, "that you are what you represent yourself to be. You have means, you are a bachelor, and you are a Christian. Well—my questions are not, as you say, conventional, but Celia is my grand-niece, and will have my money when my husband and I are called away. It is no small thing you are seeking."

"I am aware of it," he replied. "I am glad for your sake that your money is not a small thing."

This he should not have said, because it was impolitic.

"I have one question more to ask you," said

Mrs. Pontifex, drawing herself more upright than ever. "You are, I understand, some sixty years of age."

"I am sixty-two," he replied blandly. "It is my great misfortune to have been born forty-four years before Miss Celia Tyrrell."

"Then in the name of goodness," she cried, "what on earth do you want with a young wife? You are only three years younger than I. You might just as well ask *me* to marry you."

"My dear!" cried John Pontifex, in natural alarm.

"I cannot, madam," Herr Räumer replied,—"however much one might desire such a consummation.—I cannot ask you in the very presence of your husband."

Everybody laughed, including Celia, and Aunt Jane drew herself up proudly.

"You disgraceful man," she said. "How dare you say such things to me! If John Pontifex were not in Holy Orders I should expect him to—to—"

"I fear I should do so, my dear," John Pontifex interposed. "I am sure in fact, that, without the

—ahem!—the deterrent influence of my cloth, I should do so."

"I am unfortunate this evening," the German went on, still bland and smiling. "I am advanced in years. All the more reason why a young lady —of Christian principles—should assist me in passing those years pleasantly."

"Pleasantly?" she echoed. "Is all you think of —to pass the last years of your life pleasantly? Would I allow my husband to pass his time in mere pleasantness?"

"You would not, my dear," said John Pontifex, firmly.

"Mere pleasantness: a Fool's Paradise. George and Clara Tyrrell, I am your aunt, and entitled, I believe, to be heard."

"Surely," said Mr. Tyrrell. "Pray say what you think."

Celia laid her hand on her aunt's arm.

"Dear Aunt Jane," she said, "Herr Räumer has done me the very great honour of asking me to be his wife. He has also very kindly consented not to press for an answer. I feel—I am sure he feels himself—the many difficulties in the way. And if those difficulties prove insuperable, I trust to his generosity—his generosity as a gentleman—not to press me any longer."

"To be sure," said Aunt Jane, "people can always be put off. We can tell them that Herr Räumer felt for you the affection of a grandfather."

The German winced for a moment.

"Thank you, dear Mrs. Pontifex," he said. "You would smooth all the difficulties for us, I am sure."

He shrugged his shoulders.

"Let us have no more explanations. I have to thank Celia—Miss Tyrrell—for putting the position of things clearly. If she cannot see her way to accepting my addresses—there is an end—and things"—looking at Mr. Tyrrell—"must take their own course. If she can, she will have in me a devoted husband who will be proud to belong to the families of Tyrrell and Pontifex."

Aunt Jane was not, however, to be mollified. She kissed Celia on the forehead. "You are a sensible girl, my dear, and you will know how to refuse a man old enough to be your grandfather,"—then she gathered her skirts together. "George and Clara Tyrrell, when you have got over this folly, we shall be glad to see you at our house again. If it comes to anything further I shall alter my will. John Pontifex, I am ready."

She swept out of the room followed by her husband.

Then Mrs. Tyrrell sat up and began to express her indignation.

"When young people desire to marry," she said to her future son-in-law, who was not much more than twenty years older than herself, "they speak to each other, and then to their parents. That is regular, I believe?"

"Quite regular," said the Herr.

"When they have asked each other, and then spoken to the parents," she went on, exhausting the subject, "what else remains to be said?"

"Clearly nothing."

"There certainly is a difference in age," said the good lady, "but if Celia does not mind that——"

"Quite so," he interrupted.

"Religion, too, the same," she went on.

"Actually a coincidence in religion."

"Then what Aunt Jane meant by going off in

that way, I cannot conceive. The very best tea-things, too!"

"My dear mamma," said Celia, "the conversation is useless. I am not engaged to Herr Räumer."

Nothing more was said, and the lover presently withdrew.

Mr. Tyrrell led me downstairs to his own office.

There he took the step common among Englishmen who are anxious and nervous, especially when they want to deaden repentance. He drank a tumbler and a half of brandy and water strong.

"I wish he was dead, Laddy," he murmured; "I wish he was dead."

"Can you do nothing?"

"I can put him off—I can gain time—and perhaps something will happen. If not, she *must* marry him. She must. Else——"

He finished his glass of brandy and water.

"She must not. Face anything rather than bring such a fate upon your daughter."

"Face anything," he repeated. "What do you know about it?"

"At least, I know that there is nothing in common with him and your daughter."

"What have I in common with my wife? Stuff and nonsense. What has any man in common with his wife? The husband and the wife lead different lives. When they are together in what they call society, they pretend. Rubbish about things in common."

"Then look at the difference of age."

"So much the better, Ladislas," said Mr. Tyrrell, fiercely. I hardly knew him to-night in this unusual mood. "So much the better. He will die soon perhaps; the sooner the better."

"Will he treat her kindly?"

"They will live in this town. I shall watch them. If he ill-treats my little girl—my pretty Celia—I will—I will—but that is nonsense. He will make her his plaything."

"Is that what Celia looks for in marriage?"

"Will you have some brandy and water? No. I take it now, just for the present while this business worries me, to steady the nerves."

He mixed himself another tumbler.

"Why, Ladislas," he resumed his talk, "how

foolishly you talk. One would think you were a girl. What Celia looks for in marriage! What is the use of looking for anything, either from marriage or anything else in this world? Disappointment we shall get—never doubt it—and punishment for mistakes—never doubt that. Probably also bad men, unscrupulous men, will get a hold of you, and make you do things you would rather afterwards not have done.

"If I had the key of that safe," he murmured, sinking into a chair; "if I only had the key of that safe"—it was the small fireproof safe, with Herr Räumer's name upon it—"Celia should be free."

I came away, sick and sorry. I had heard enough, and more than enough. I knew it all along. My poor Celia!

"If I had the key of that safe!"

Then it occurred to me that the German must have it somewhere. I went to bed, and dreamed that I was prowling round and round his room, looking for a key which I could not find.

CHAPTER V.

THE CONSPIRATOR.

THE Polish question was not forgotten. In truth, it was not easy altogether to forget it. The burning fervour of Wassielewski, his glorious indifference to the probabilities of death, his scorn of failure provided the sacred fire was kept burning, all this could not but impress the imagination. When I thought of them my heart burned within me, and it seemed for the time a light thing to join my countrymen, and march with them to certain death, if only to show the world that Poland was living yet. Celia thought this kind of patriotism, this carrying on of a vendetta from father to son, was unworthy. But I never could get her to see the beauty of war, even in the palmy days of Crimean victory.

I laid my case before her, as much as I knew of it, then but little the loss of my inheritance, the death of my father, my long line of brave progenitors, the obligations of a name.

She could not be persuaded.

"You are not a soldier, Laddy," she said. "You are a musician and an artist. It is not for you to go fighting. And think of all the misery that you and I have seen. Why does not every man resolve that he for one will not fight unless he has to defend himself? Be one of the peacemakers. After all, you foolish boy, it is not you that the Russians have injured, and you have grown up an Englishman. Why, you cannot even speak your own language."

"Wassielewski will be my interpreter."

"Poor old Wassielewski! He will run against the first Russian bayonet he meets, and be killed at the very beginning."

That was, indeed, just what the old man would do. He came to see me one day, with eyes full of fervour, and a voice trembling with excitement.

"Come out, Ladislas, I have much to say to you."

He took me into St. Faith's Square, a large irregular place, with the red brick church at one end. He dragged out of his pocket a pile of papers and letters tied round with ribbon. It struck me disagreeably that Herr Räumer was walking on the other side of the Square.

"They are all with us," he whispered. "See, here are the men from Exeter, here are the London men, here are the Paris men, we have emissaries in Vienna and in Rome; for the present, the country is kept quiet, no suspicions are awakened yet; no movement of Russian troops has been made towards Poland; we shall strike a desperate blow this time."

I mechanically took the papers which he gave me to read. There were lists of names, copies of compromising letters, mysterious notes dated Paris, Vienna, Rome. This old enthusiast was a sort of Head Centre, or, at least, a confidential and trusted agent of a wide-spread conspiracy. My heart sank when I saw my own name at the head of a long list.

"The plan of the campaign is being considered. I have sent in my ideas. They are, after making a feint in Warsaw, to——"

We will not follow the conspirator's plans through all its details. I thought five years later, when the rising of 1863 took place, of Wassielewski's projected campaign, and for my country's sake regretted that they had not been adopted.

"In a very short time—it may be to-morrow—it may be in six months—we shall receive our orders to move."

"And am I to see no one first—to obey orders blindly?"

"Not blindly, Ladislas Pulaski. I shall be with you."

I suppose there was something of uncertainty in my face, for he quickly added:

"You shall see some of our people before you go. Ladislas, your heart is not yet wholly with us. I have seen that all along. It is my fault. I ought to have educated you from the beginning into hatred of the Muscovite. There ought to have been no single day in which you should not have recited the catechism of Poland's wrongs. My fault—mine."

"Forgive me, Wassielewski."

"But another day of retribution is coming. There

will be another massacre of Polish patriots to rouse Poland out of her sleep, and fill the hearts of Polish women with renewed hatred. You and I shall be among the slain, and yet you do not rejoice."

He looked forward to his own death with exultation, much as a Christian martyr brought before Nero may have looked to the cross or the stake, with the fiery fervour of a confessor who glorifies the faith. And he lamented that I, fifty years younger than himself, with no personal memories of struggle and of wrong, could not rise to his level of self-sacrifice.

"I do not rejoice, Wassielewski. I have no wish, not the slightest, to be killed, even for Poland."

He groaned.

"You *must* wish. You must go with me as I go, ready to be killed—because we shall not succeed this time—for the cause. You must feel as I feel. The others think we shall not fail; they know nothing; those of us who have better information know that Russia is too strong. I want to take you with me knowing all. I pray, night and morning, that you may come to me of your own accord, saying, 'Son of Roman Pulaski and the Lady Claudia, I belong to Poland.'"

I was deeply moved by the old man's eagerness.

"What can I say, Wassielewski? When I am with you my spirit leaps up at your words. Helpless hunchback as I am, I am ready to go with you and do what you command. Away from you, my patriotism is feeble, and I care little for Poland. Forgive me, but I tell you the simple truth."

"There is one thing I have never told you. I meant to keep it till I landed you on the sacred soil of Poland. But I will tell you now. No; not now. I must go home and think before I can tell you that. Come to me to-morrow at this time, to my room, where you and I can talk alone. You will need to be alone with me when you hear all, Ladislas Pulaski—with that knowledge ringing in your brain, the scales will fall from your eyes and you shall see."

What was he to tell me? Were there not horrors enough that I had heard already? Men beaten to death; men tortured by the knout; men sent by thousands into exile; women insulted; brides robbed of their bridegrooms, mothers of their sons;

was there one single outrage in the long list of possible crimes that had not been committed in that dark story of Polish revolt and Russian repression? Needs must, but war brings misery. The annals of the world are red with tears of blood; "woe to the conquered" is the inevitable law; but such woe, such tears, such misery, as fell upon Poland by the will of the Czar are surely unequalled since the days when a conquered people all fell by the sword, or were led away to a hopeless servitude. What more had Wassielewski to tell me?

By some strange irony I always met Herr Räumer after Wassielewski had been with me. That same evening, as I came home from a walk with Celia, I was saluted by him. He looked down upon me with his white shaggy eyebrows and his green spectacles, as if half in pity, half in contempt. In his presence I felt a very small conspirator indeed.

"I saw you this morning," he said, "walking and talking with your old rebel, Wassielewski. Brave old man! Energetic old man! Useful to his friends. And, oh! how useful to his country!"

Nothing could surpass the intense scorn in his voice.

"He is getting up another little rebellion, I gather from certain Cracow papers. At least, there are indications of another rising, and it is not likely that Wassielewski will be out of it. Such a chance does not come often."

"You mean, such a chance for Poland?"

"No—I mean for a conspirator. You do not understand—how can you?—the charm of rebellion. Once a rebel—always a rebel. It is like acting. Those who have faced the footlights once are always wanting to go on again. Wassielewski is seventy years of age, and for sixty, or thereabouts, has been conspiring. It would have been a good thing for Poland had some one knocked him on the head when he first began. And a good thing for you."

"Why for me?"

"Because Roman Pulaski would still be living and still be a great proprietor in Poland; because you would have been, as he was, a friend and *protégé* of the Imperial Court."

"How do you know so much about me?"

He laughed.

"I have read current history. I read, and I remember. And I know the story of Roman Pulaski. It was Wassielewski who took your father from his quiet chateau, and launched him on the stormy waters of rebellion. Thank him, then, not Russia, for all your misfortunes. You ought to be very grateful to that old man."

This was a new view of the case, and, for the moment, a staggerer.

"That is for the past, Ladislas Pulaski. Now for the future."

"What of the future?"

"It is a Paradise of Fools. In the Future Poland will be restored; there will be no more wars; nationalities will not be repressed in the Future——"

"At all events, it is better to believe in the Future than in the Present."

"You think so? That is because you are young. I believe in the Present because I am old. I love the Present, and work for it. When I am dead people may say of me what they like, and may do what they like. That is their own business. I eat well; I drink good wine; I read French novels; I smoke excellent tobacco: what more can the Future give me? Your friend Wassielewski fought once for the Future. He gets tenpence a day for his reward; he fiddles for sailors; he conspires for Poland; he will die in some obscure field leading peasants armed with scythes against Russian troops armed with rifles."

"I would rather be Wassielewski than——"

"Than I? *Ca va sans dire.* You are young," he laughed, and showed his white teeth. "Meantime, remember what I told you. Where there are three conspirators there is one traitor. Have nothing to do with them; refuse to be murdered for Poland; go on with your music-lessons—anything you like—but do not join conspiracies."

He seemed to know everything, this man. For the first time a strange thought crossed my brain. Could he have *received* intelligence of the intended rising?

"I mean well by you, Ladislas Pulaski, although you suspect me, and do not love me. That does not matter. I wish to see you kept out of the fatal business which killed your father."

"Crack-brained idiots!" he ejaculated. "There is in the Kremlin a box. In the box is a most valuable document, shown to strangers as a curiosity. It is the Constitution of Poland. Reflect upon that fact. Again, there is outside Cracow a mound erected in immortal memory of Kosciusko. It is a mound so high that it dominates the town. Therefore, the Austrians have turned it into a fort by which, if necessary, to crush the town. That is another inspiriting fact for a Pole to consider."

"It is like the Austrians."

"Doubtless. Otherwise they would not have built their fort. You would have preferred seeing them sympathise with the fallen hero. England and France have made of Poland a beautiful theme for the most exalted sentiments and speeches. But they do not fight for Poland. Voltaire, who did not share in the general enthusiasm, even wrote a burlesque poem on the Poles. Then England put clauses in the Treaty of 1815 to ensure the government of the country by her Constitution. When Nicholas laughed at the clauses and tore up the treaty, England and France did not fight. Who keeps treaties when he is strong enough to break them? Who goes to war for a broken treaty when he is not strong enough? What does the new Czar say to the Poles? 'No dreams, gentlemen.' It is a dream to believe that Poland is not abandoned. It is a dream that a few madmen can get up a successful rebellion. *Finis Poloniæ!*"

He inhaled a tremendous volume of smoke, and sent it up in the air in a thick cloud.

"Look——There goes the liberty of Poland. Say I well, Ladislas Pulaski?"

"No," I replied, bluntly.

"Did you ever hear what a great Pole said when they wanted him to conspire? '*Mourir pour la patrie? Oui, je comprend cela; mais y vivre? Jamais.*' And he did neither."

I was filled with strange forebodings; with that feeling of expectancy which sometimes comes over one at moments when there seems impending the stroke of Fate; I could not rest; wild dreams crossed my brain. Nor was Celia happier. We wandered backwards and forwards in the leafy and shady retreat, restless and unhappy. The great elms about us were bright with their early foliage of sweet young June; the birds were flying about among the branches where they were never disturbed; the thrush with his low and cheerful note, surely the most contented among birds; the blackbird with his carol, a bird of sanguine temperament; the blue tit, the robin, the chaffinch—we knew every one of them by sight because we saw them every day. And the meadows at the foot of the walls were bright with golden cups.

"How can I give it up, Cis?" I asked.

She answered with her sweet sad smile. We had both been brooding in silence.

"I am selfish," she said. "I think of nothing but my own troubles. You must not give it up, Laddy. You belong here, to the Captain, and to me. You must not go out among strangers."

I shook my head.

"Wassielewski says I must. It would be hard to tear myself away, Cis—not to talk to you ever again, to see you no more."

"Why no more, Laddy?"

"I am to give more than my presence to the revolt, Cis. I am to give what Wassielewski gives—my life."

Just then we saw him marching along the

ramparts towards us. His eyes were upon us, but he saw nothing. He came nearer and nearer, but he took no notice; he swung his arms violently to and fro; his long white hair streamed behind him in the wind; he carried his black felt hat in one hand; he halted when he came to the wall of the bastion, leaned for a moment upon the rampart, gazing fixedly out upon the bright waters of the harbour. What did he see there? Then he turned and faced us, but spoke as if he saw us not.

"The time is at hand," he murmured, in the low tones of a prophet. "The wolves and the ravens may gather in the woods and wait for the dead. The mothers shall array their sons—the wives shall buckle the sword for their husbands, the daughters for their lovers; once in every generation the sacrifice of the bravest and noblest, till the time comes; till then the best must die."

"Not Ladislas," cried Celia, throwing herself in front of me. "Take any one else, take whom you please to be murdered. But you shall not take my brother Ladislas."

He made no answer; I suppose he did not hear. Presently he stepped lightly from the breastwork, and walked slowly away, still waving his arms in a sort of triumph.

"He is mad, Laddy," Celia whispered. "You must not trust your fate to a madman."

"He is only mad sometimes, Cis. It is when he thinks too much about the past."

"Laddy, if you go away and leave me; if Leonard —but that is impossible. God will be good to us— yet. I could not bear my life without you."

"Tell me, Cis dear, has he pressed for an answer?"

She shook her head.

"It is not that," she said. "He is patient. But it is my father. Do not put my thoughts into words, Laddy. They are too dreadful. And my mother sees nothing."

CHAPTER VI.

WASSIELEWSKI'S SECRET.

THE Polish newspapers at one time, and until they were ordered to desist, used to print the words Past and Future in very big capitals, while they spoke of the present in the smallest possible type. That was Wassielewski's method. The Past was radiant with Polish glory and Polish struggles set in a black background of Russian atrocities. Like one of the new-fashioned "Arrangements in Brown," the details were smudged. The Future, after a good deal more of fighting and bloodshed, was also to be a chronicle of great glory. As for the present it did not exist, it was a dream.

For himself he was almost the last of the Poles whom I remembered as a child in the old black barrack. The barrack itself was gone, and the Poles dispersed. Those who were left lived about the town singly. Wassielewski alone among them still nourished thoughts of revenge and patriotism. He was certainly the only man of all the exiled Poles capable of giving life to the cause in a hopeless effort, where the only object was to keep alive the spark of rebellion. He also never flagged or lost heart, because he knew what he had to give, and he knew what he was going to get. I was accustomed to his fanaticism. If he met me when I was a child, he was wont to say, parenthetically, "Ladislas, Poland is not dead, but sleeping," and then pass on without waiting for an answer. He was like a bird which has but one tune; his one idea was the resuscitation of his country. Sometimes he would stop me in the street, and take off his hat, standing like a prophet of Israel with his deep-set eyes, his long white locks, and his passionate look, keeping me beside him while he whispered in earnest tones, "Listen, Ladislas Pulaski, there is a stir in her limbs. She will spring to her feet again, and call upon her children to arise and fight. Then let all the Poles scattered over the broad face of the earth, the Poles of Gallicia, the Poles of the Kingdom, join together. We are the children of those who fought with Kosciusko, and we are the grandchildren of those who followed Sobieski. If we die, the tradition of hate will be preserved. Let us die, if Heaven so will it."

I was therefore trained in the traditional hatred of Russia, almost as much as if I had been brought up in Warsaw among those Polish ladies who go in mourning all their days, and refuse to dance or have any joy. But my own feeling was of the passive kind, which is not fertile in action. By temperament as well as physique I was inclined to the contemplative life; if I regarded the Muscovite with patriotic hatred, I was by no means prepared to leave my own ease, and put on the armour of a soldier. Besides, to all intents I was an Englishman, with English ideas, English prejudices; and the Poles were foreigners to me, although I was of Polish blood, and—I was a cripple.

Wassielewski saw with pity that his most fiery denunciations, his most highly-coloured narratives of blood failed to rouse me to the level of his own enthusiasm, and therefore the old conspirator had recourse to his last and most desperate measure. If that failed I was hopeless. He told me the secret that had been religiously kept from me by the Captain, Mr. Broughton, and the few who knew it—the tragedy of my birth.

I wish he had not told me; I ought to have been spared the bitter knowledge; it was with kindness that it had been kept from me. For the story fired my blood, and maddened me for awhile with the thirst of vengeance.

It was about four o'clock one afternoon—a week before Leonard's return, that I went to Wassielewski's lodgings—at his own request. I went unwillingly, because it pained me to see him so eager, and to feel myself so lukewarm over the wrongs of my country; but I went.

His one room was furnished with a narrow bed, a chair, a table, and a music-stand. A crucifix was hanging on the wall—Wassielewski was a Catholic—a sword hung below it; at the head of the bed was a portrait in water-colours, which I had never seen before, of a young lady, dressed in the fashion of the Thirties. She had a sweet, calm face, and her eyes, which fell upon me when I entered the room, seemed to follow me about. They were large eyes full of thought and love.

"That is your mother, Ladislas Pulaski," said the old man slowly. "Your sainted mother, one of the martyrs of Poland. Claudia, wife of Roman Pulaski."

My mother! I, who never knew a mother, and hardly ever gave her memory one filial thought. A strange yearning came over me as I gazed at the face, and saw it blurred through the tears that crowded in my eye.

"My mother! Wassielewski, why have you never shown this to me before?"

"Because I waited for the moment to come when I could give you her portrait, tell you her story, and send you forth to kill Russians in revenge. Sit down, poor boy. I have much to say, and nothing that is not sad."

I sat down with strange forebodings. But I took the portrait of my mother from the wall.

"You will give this to me, Wassielewski?"

"When I die, or when we go together to Poland."

Ah! The tender sweetness of the face; the kind face; the noble face. Ah! the good and true eyes that saw her son after so many years; so bright, and yet so sad. For they had the sadness which seems to lie in the eyes of all whom death takes young. Death! How did my mother die? And while I looked I felt that the poor old man who loved her so much—else he could not have been so careful for me—was looking with me in her face, and dropping tears upon my head.

"Do not tell me, Wassielewski—not now—if it pains you so much."

"That will pain you more," he groaned. "Day and night for twenty years it has been ever before my eyes. I was only her humble friend and servant. You are her son. How shall I tell you the shameful story?

"Sit so, Ladislas Pulaski, with your eyes upon the face of your dead mother—perhaps she will smile upon you as she does upon me sometimes in moonlit nights when I lie awake and listen for the call from Poland. So—so—while I try to tell you how she died, and how your father died."

His voice was calm and steady, but his eyes were wild. I looked at him no more, but kept my eyes upon the picture, awed and expectant.

He took his violin from the case, and played a few bars walking up and down the room.

"That is a Polish waltz. We used to dance a great deal in Poland before 1830. We were Russian subjects, it is true, but we were happier than our brothers who were under Prussia. Some of us were young, too—not I. I am seventy-five now, and I am talking of events which took place only five-and-twenty years ago. But I was not too old to join in the dances of the people. And I was happy in my stewardship of the Lady Claudia. She was an only child, like your father, Roman Pulaski, and I was the steward of her father, and had special charge of the young lady. There is a girl in this place; I often see you with her."

"Celia Tyrrell?"

"Yes—perhaps. She has the eyes of your mother and her sweet face. I think she must be good, like her.

"Lady Claudia was not proud. We went about together, her father and she and I, to all the peasants' festivals. I was but a peasant born, but she, it is true—oh! she was a great lady. When we had a wedding it lasted a week, and we danced all night; we wore our national dress; we sang our national songs—this was one of them."

He played a quaint delightful air, full of sweetness and character.

"We ate our *bigos* and *cholodiec;* we laughed and joked. And with the Muscovites we were friends. You would have been a happy child, Ladislas Pulaski, could you have been brought up among your own people, and learned their customs—such as they were. Now, it is all changed. The national costume is forbidden; we may not sing the Polish hymns——Listen to one. Ah! you cannot understand the words."

He played a hymn with soft and melancholy cadences, crooning rather than singing the words which I could not, as he said, understand.

"We dance no longer; even the young Polish girls, who loved dancing more than any girls in the world, dance no more; we go in mourning all our days;—even the young Polish girls, whose dress was so gay and bright, wear black all their lives; we laugh no more, but sit with weeping eyes; we go to church, not to pray for good harvests and joy, but for the hour of revenge."

He paused a moment.

"That is what you know already. Up to the age of nineteen, my young lady was as happy as the day is long. She was as happy as God ever allowed any human being to be. For when she was eighteen she was married—to your father.

"Roman Pulaski was worthy of her—he, alone among men. He was of a good descent; he was as rich, he was as handsome, he was as strong and brave as she was true and good. They were married, and you were born—a strong and straight-backed boy—a true Pulaski, with curly brown hair, and plenty of it, when you were but a little baby. And who so happy as your mother? All day long she held you in her arms; all day and all night; it made the tears come into my eyes only to see how pleased and happy she was with her child.

"That lasted two years. Then came the insurrection. Of course your father joined it. How could he keep out of it? And the Lady Claudia wove silk banners, and brought her jewels to buy arms, and gave all she had to the brave rebels.

"One day, after three months of fighting, I came back—alone. Your father had disappeared; our men were all killed; and the Russians were marching upon the castle to destroy it. I remembered how, once, they set fire to a house full of Poles, and killed all who tried to escape. So I hurried your mother away; we carried the child between us, and escaped into the woods, where we wandered backwards and forwards through the bitter cold night, and watched at nightfall the red glow in the sky, which marked our burning castle. So you no longer had a house, you and the Lady Claudia.

"In the morning, finding that the Cossacks were gone, I took her home to our village. It was a place full of women and children; not a man left in it; only a few boys of ten and old men of seventy; but because there were no men, I thought she would be safe. She was brave—always brave—and in her pale face there was no thought of repentance. They weighed the cost, and joined the losing side. Her husband gone—perhaps dead; her house destroyed; nothing left in the world but her year-old child. Yet she never lamented. Only the second day, she sent me away. 'Old friend,' she said, 'Go—and, if you can, bring me news of Roman Pulaski. If he is dead we will mourn for him as those who mourn for the dead in Christ.'

"I left her—in safety, as I thought—I crept cautiously through the woods, from village to village, and asked of the women and old men in each place for news. For a time I could learn nothing, but one day I found a newspaper, and read that Roman Pulaski was not dead but a prisoner.

"It would have been better for him had he died in battle. You have heard—I have told you over and over again—how the Czar Nicholas hated the very name of Pole; how there was no cruelty practised by his officers, no severity so great, towards the Poles that it should displease him. But the case of one who stood so high as your father was too important to be decided upon even by the Archduke Constantine's favourite, General Kuruta.

Roman Pulaski had been a favourite in the St. Petersburg Court; he had attracted the notice of the Empress, who hoped to attach him to the Russian cause; his rebellion incensed the Czar more than the defection of all the other Poles put together. Imagine, therefore, his satisfaction at having his enemy in his own power. At first he ordered that the prisoner should be shot. This order was immediately afterwards commuted, as he called it, to hard labour in the mines of Siberia for life, which was called the Czar's clemency.

"Even the Russians were appalled at such a sentence, which condemned a gentleman to the lowest degradation of companionship with criminals. They drew up a petition; it was represented that the Count Roman Pulaski was young and hot-headed; they said he had been drawn into the rebellion by disaffected advisers and by misrepresentations. The Czar refused to receive the petition. Then the Empress herself, his own wife, threw herself on her knees at his feet and implored mercy.

"'You ask mercy for a Pole,' he cried. 'Then this is what you shall get for him.' He took the paper containing the sentence, and added to it *in his own handwriting*. 'And the prisoner shall walk the whole way.'"

"Walk?—walk the whole way from Warsaw to Siberia?"

"Walk. Think of it quietly if you can, for a while. Try to understand something of what it means. To be one of a gang of murderers and common thieves, because they did not allow him to perform his journey with brother Poles; to step side by side, manacled together at the wrist, with one of the worst of these criminals; to sleep with him at night on a sloping bench; to eat and drink with him; never to be separated from him; to be driven along the never-ending road by Cossacks armed with whips; to endure every indignity of blows and curses; to have no rest by day, no repose by night; to eat the vilest and commonest food; to spend the winter—it was in the winter that he started—pacing for ever along the white and frozen snow; to be on the road when spring returned; to be still walking always with the thieves and murderers, in the glaring summer.

"Take a map, measure the distance from Warsaw to Moscow, from Moscow to Astrakhan, from Astrakhan to Tobolski, and thence to the mines. You will say to yourself, Fifteen miles a day;

that makes—how many months of walking? Left behind him a wife, young and beautiful as the day; a boy not old enough yet to do more than look in his father's face, and cry, 'Papa—Wassielewski!'

"Wife and boy gone—happiness gone for ever—no hope—before him the long road with the horrible daily and nightly companions, and after the road? Perhaps after the road the worst part of the sentence; for in the road there is change, in the mines none; day after day the same work; day after day the same hopeless toil; day after day the same gloom; day after day the same wretched fellow-prisoners; the same faces; the death in life.

"They used to go mad, some of them; they used to commit suicide; some would murder a soldier or a gaoler for the mere excitement of being flogged to death. Some tried to run away. It was fortunate for those who made their escape in winter, because when night fell they lay down in the snow—out on the free white snow, which covered them up and hid them after the cold winter wind had fanned them to sleep, and when they were found in the spring they were dead corpses.

covered over with tall grasses and pitiful flowers. Those who neither went mad, nor were knouted, nor were frozen to death, nor committed suicide, dropped away and died day by day, like your father, and for the last few months of their lives, God, more merciful than the Czar, made them stupid."

Wassielewski stopped. I looked up at him with beating heart and flashing eyes. His own eyes, deep-set and stern, were glowing with the intensity of his wrath, and the red gash on his cheek was a long white line.

"Go on, Wassielewski," I cried, "tell me more."

"I have thought upon that journey," he continued in a calm voice, "till I seem to know it every step. And he was so tall, so brave, so handsome.

"News came, later on not for a long time—about him. More than half the convicts died upon the road, the man to whom he was manacled threw himself down upon the road one day, and refused to move another step; they flogged him till he could not have walked if he had tried; but he still refused, and then they flogged him again until he died. That was part of the Czar's clemency. Your father was one of the few who survived the journey, and reached Siberia in safety. He sent home by a sure hand a little wooden cross, on which he had carved—the names of Claudia his wife, and Ladislas his boy."

"Stop—stop! Wassielewski, I cannot bear it."

"I shall not stop," he replied, "you must bear this, and more. There is worse to hear. Do you think it is for nothing that I tell you all these things? The cross was to show his wife that he was alive, and that he still thought of them. But when it arrived his wife was dead, and the child was in exile. The cross,"—he opened a little cabinet which stood upon a chest of drawers—"the cross is here. I have kept it for you."

It was a roughly-carved cross, eighteen inches long, of a dark-grained wood, a Latin cross. On the longer limb was carved in letters rude, but deeply cut in the wood, "Roman to Claudia," and on the transverse limb the single word, "Ladislas."

"See, from his grave your father calls you."

"From his grave?"

"He died, like all the prisoners in the mines, of hard work, of despair, of misery, and neglect. He could write no letters, he could receive none; he had no longer anything to hope for in this world. Roman Pulaski died. Grey, deaf, and blind, my poor old master died. He was not thirty years of age.

"When he was dead, lying news was published in the papers by the command of Nicholas. They said that he had been released from the mines, that he had voluntarily entered as a private soldier in a Caucasian regiment, that he had fallen in action. Lies! Lies! No one believed them. As if Roman Pulaski would not have written to Poland for news of his wife and son; as if he would not have flown along the road as soon as he obtained his liberty, to learn if they were dead or living. No! In the darkest and deepest mine with the foulest thieves of a Muscovite crowd, Roman Pulaski lived out his wretched years, and died his wretched death. And you are his son.

"Before you go home, remember this: he died

for Poland; his death is not forgotten; for fifty generations, if need be, the story shall be told of the Czar's revenge."

He paused for a moment.

CHAPTER VII.

THE MASSACRE OF THE INNOCENTS.

"I HAVE more to tell you," he went on, wiping the beads from his brow wearily. "More to tell you, more that I cannot tell without the bitterest pain, and that will sadden all your after years. But you must learn it, you must learn it, before you become a true child of Poland."

He leant over me and kissed my head.

"Poor boy! I thought at one time that you might be spared. The good Captain said to me when you went away to live with him, 'Let him not know, Wassielewski, let him never know.' I said, 'He shall never know, Captain; no one shall tell him:—unless his country ask for him. Then he shall know, because the knowledge will fire the blood, and make him fight like ten men. We are all like ten men when we rise to fight the Muscovite.' So I promised and I prayed of a night to the Lady Claudia, who is now a saint in Heaven, and hears what sinners ask, that she would guard her son from harm. 'Because,' I said on my knees, 'he is not a strong man like your husband or your servant; he is afflicted, he is feeble, he is a boy of peace and fond of music, and he has made good friends.' I knelt by the bed, and I looked on that face.

"The face changed as I prayed, and sometimes, by candlelight, or by moonlight, I could see the eyes of my mistress shining upon me, or see her lips move as if to speak or to smile. And always happy. Ladislas, happy are those who forgive."

"But we cannot forgive," I said.

"Never, boy, never. We are God's instruments of wrath. And now the time has come, and Poland asks for you. So I *must* tell you, Ladislas," he added, pitifully, "I must tell you, in addition, how your mother died. You will think over the story every day for the rest of your life. And you will understand, henceforth, how Russia may become the Protector of Christians—out of her own country.

"It happened while I was away, looking for certain news of your father. I left her in safety, as I thought, among the women and children. Even I did not know how far the Czar could carry his revenge. Not even the little children were safe. An order came from St. Petersburg that all orphan Polish children—all those whose fathers had fallen in the insurrection—all who were a burden to the State—should be carried away and brought up in military schools. That was a master-stroke. The little Poles were to become Russians, to fight their brothers.

"You were not an orphan, nor a burden on the State; you did not fall within that law. It was by the great, by the divine clemency of the Czar that that ukase was issued, to save the children whom every Polish household would have welcomed, to relieve the State of a burden which did not exist. But the order did not affect you, and if I had known of it I should not have been disturbed. You were safe, safe with your mother, and she was safe among her own people, the women who knew her and loved her.

"As the order was issued it had to be carried out, and the soldiers were sent to find orphan children, begging their bread, and a burden on the State. But there were none; yet the order must be obeyed. So they began to carry off all the children they could find, whether they were orphans or not, whether their mothers wept and shrieked, or whether they sat silent, struck with the mad stupor of a misfortune greater than they could bear.

"When Herod slew the infants in Bethlehem, there were some thirty killed. When Nicholas murdered the innocents in Poland, there were thousands. Perhaps, when one crime becomes as well known as the other, that of the Czar will take its proper rank.

"In the afternoon, when the day was sinking, there came clattering up to the village where your mother had taken refuge a long cavalcade of carts, horses, and cavalry. In the carts were infants;—it was a day of winter, and the snow was lying over the fields and in the branches of the pines.

The carts were covered, it is true, and within them the children cried and moaned, huddled together against each other for warmth ; some mere infants in arms ; some five or six years of age, who carried the smaller ones ; some little toddling things of two. They had spread rough blankets on the floors of the carts, but still the helpless babes were cold. And their only nurses were the soldiers, who had small pity.

"The women of the village came out crying over the poor children, bringing them bread and milk. With them they carried their own. They had better have stayed in-doors ; better still have fled into the woods, and hidden there till the Cossacks went away. For presently, the soldiers began picking up the children of the village and tossing them, too, into their carts. Among them, led by an older child, wrapped in furs, was a little boy of two years old——you, Ladislas Pulaski.

"You were straight-backed then, poor boy ; straight and comely, like your father——

"When they rode away, the carts lumbering along the roads, the children crying, the soldiers swearing, they were followed by a stream of women, who shrieked and cried, and first among them all ran and cried your mother—the Lady Claudia. Yes—she was brave when her beautiful home was burned with all the sweet things she had grown up amongst; but when she saw the boy torn from her, she became, they told me, like a mad woman. They were all mad women.

"It was twenty-four hours later when I returned and heard what had happened. The carts had all that much start of me; also I had to be careful, because near the villages I might be recognised and arrested. I followed on the high-road when I could—through forests when I could find a faithful guide—anyhow so that I followed.——After two days of pursuit, I found — courage, Ladislas — courage, boy—so—drink this water—lie down for a moment—sob and cry—it will do you good as it did me, when I found her—the tale is almost told.

"I found her lying cold and dead in the road. She was bareheaded, and her long hair lay blown about her beautiful head; her face was looking with its pale cold cheeks and closed eyes—looking still along the road in the direction of the carts—

one arm was bent under her, one hand upon her heart; one lay extended, the fingers clutched in the snow, as if she would drag herself along the way by which she could no longer creep; her shoes had fallen from her feet, she was frozen;—in the night she had fallen, and, too weak to rise, must have died in the painless sleep that swiftly closes the eyes of those who lie down in our winter snow. I lifted her and bore her to the edge of the forest, where, because I could not dig her a grave, I made a hole in the snow, and covered her over with branches to keep off the wolves. I knelt by her dead form and called Heaven to witness that such revenge as I could work upon the people who had killed her I would work—it is a vow which I have renewed from day to day; and, after many years, the time has come at last. It always comes to those who have faith and patience.

"When I had buried your mother, I hurried along the road still in pursuit of the train of children. These trains do not move quickly, and I knew that I should come up with it—sooner or later. The roads were very still and quiet; it was not only the snow that lay on the earth, but the dread and terror of the Cossacks. Death was in the air; in the woods lay the bodies of the men: in the villages lay the women weeping; on the cold roads lumbered the long lines of kibitkas that carried away the children. Somewhere on that road marched the train of convicts manacled wrist to wrist, your father among them.

"Presently—it may have been a day, it may have been an hour, after I left your dead mother, I heard far off the dull dead sound of the carts, the cracking of whips and the curses of the drivers. Then I stopped to think. If they saw me I should be shot, and that would be of no use to any one. Now, if I lost sight altogether of the train, how could I help you, who were in it?

"Walking and running, I kept up close behind the train; as the night fell again, I could get so close as to hear the wailing of the children, who cried for hunger and for cold. And Providence befriended us; for while I went along the road, I saw something move in the moonlight, and heard a faint cry. Ladislas, it was you. You had fallen from the cart, and they left you there to die. Perhaps they did not see you. Five minutes more, and you would have died, like your mother, of that fatal sleep of frost.

"There is nothing more to tell——I had a long and weary journey from village to village before I reached the Austrian frontier, and found a friend who would help us over mountains and by forests to Switzerland. All Europe was full of our sufferings, and we made friends wherever we went; there were societies called 'Friends of Poland,' who helped us with money and work; had they given us soldiers and arms we should have asked no other help—we passed from Switzerland to France, and from France we came to England. Always the same kindness from the people; the same indignation; and the same help. I wonder, now, if they have forgotten the cause of Poland; perhaps, because it is twenty years ago.

"Well, as the days passed on, I noticed something. At first it was not much, but as the time went on, I found that your back was round, and that you were—poor boy—deformed. It was done by the fall from the cart. Remember, Ladislas, that you owe that, as well as everything else—to the Czar. When you look in the glass, say to yourself, 'But for them I should be well and straight like my father:' when you pass a rich man's house you may say, 'My house stood among woods fairer than these, with more splendid gardens; the Czar burned it, and took my broad lands.' When you stand upon the ramparts and see the lines of convicts, working, silent, in single file, think of your father dying slowly in the Siberian mines—and every evening and every morning, look at the face of your mother and think of her rushing along the frozen roads, catching at the hands of the soldiers, crying and imploring—to fall at last for very weakness on the ground and die in misery.

"Hush, boy—hush—strengthen your heart—rouse yourself—think that your arms are strong though your back is round; you can fire a gun; you can kill a Russian; you can fight, as men fight now; and you are a Pulaski.

"I thought, when I saw what you were, that Heaven had resolved to spare you the common lot of Poles. But that is not so—we must all go now."

"Yes, Wassielewski—all must go. I among the rest."

"I knew you would say that, when you had

been told all. Look me in the face, boy, and swear it."

"I swear it," I murmured, in a broken voice. "By the portrait of my mother, Wassielewski, I will go with you to Poland, when you claim my promise. You shall take me back to my own people : you shall say to them that I am poor and deformed ; that I can neither march with them, nor ride, nor stand upright among their ranks ; that I cannot even speak my own language ; but that I have greater wrongs to avenge than any of them ; and that I ask leave just to crawl among them and load my rifle with the rest."

"Good—boy—good." The old man's eyes had an infinite tenderness in their depths while he took my hand. "I am taking you to Death. That is almost certain. I pray God that we may die together, and that we may die upon a heap of Russians while the enemy is flying before our faces scattered like the chaff before the wind. Then I can take you by the hand and lead you to Heaven, where we shall find them both, waiting for us—Count Roman and Lady Claudia—and I shall say, 'My master and my mistress, I have brought your boy home to you. And he died for Poland.'

"It is not that I have done this of myself," he went on. "For years a voice has been ringing in my ears which at first I could not understand,—it was only a voice, and indistinct. Gradually I began to hear and make out what it said. 'The time is coming,' it said, 'the time is coming. Prepare to end thy work. The time is coming.' That lasted for a long while, but I was patient, because I knew that it was the Lady Claudia who spoke to me at night, and she would have good reason for what she said. And now the voice says more. It says, 'Ladislas must be told; Ladislas must go with you; let Ladislas, too, fight for Poland.' We must obey a voice from Heaven, and so I have told you.

"Remember, I can promise you nothing,—not even glory, not even a name. You may be killed in a nameless fight upon a village green; you may follow your father to Siberia; I know not. I partly read the future, but not all. I see fighting. I hear the Polish hymn; there are the accursed grey coats, there is the firing of guns, and all is finished. Among the patriots I do not see you, Ladislas, and I do not see myself."

"You have sworn, and I will give you besides

your father's cross, your mother's portrait. Take them with you to-night, put them in some safe place, pray with them in your hand, night and day. Remember, you are no longer a music-master in an English town, you are a child of Poland, and you teach music till you hear your country's call. And now, farewell; wait and expect."

* * * * * * *

"Play something, Celia, my dear," said the Captain. "Soothe his spirit with music. Poor boy, poor boy! He should not have told you."

* * * * * * *

I went home in a dream, bearing with me the precious relics which Wassielewski gave me. I think I was mad that evening. It was nine o'clock when I reached home, and Celia had waited for me all the evening. But I had no eyes for Celia, and no thought for anything but what I had heard. And then, in such language as came to me, with such passion and tears as the tale called up within me, I told my story and once more renewed my vow.

* * * * * * *

There was no sleep for me that night, but in the

morning I fell into a slumber broken by unquiet dreams. There was the lumbering, grinding roll upon the frozen snow of the children's train escorted by the mounted soldiers; there was the figure of my mother, lying stone dead on a road of ice; there was the gang of convicts limping along a road which seemed to have no beginning and no end.

* * * * * * *

They would not let me go to my pupils; my hands were hot, my brow was burning. Celia came to sit with me, and we talked and wept together. I was fain to tell my story all over again. She held my hand while I told it, and when it was finished I saw in her face no wrath, none of the madness with which Wassielewski filled my soul the day before, but only a great sadness. I was still mad for revenge, but somehow I felt instinctively as if Celia's sorrow was not a higher thing than the old Pole's thirst for revenge. And I was ashamed in presence of her sad and sympathising eyes to renew my oath of vengeance.

"Poor Laddy!" she said, "What a tale of misery and wrong! Let us pity the soldiers who had to carry out such an order. Let us believe that the Czar did not know—could not know—how his order was obeyed. Do not dwell upon it, dear. Do not let cruel and revengeful thoughts grow out of the recollection. 'Vengeance is mine,' you know. Your mother's face—how beautiful it is!—does not make you think of revenge? See how calmly the sweet eyes look at you! And oh! dear, dear, Laddy, make no more rash vows, at least till Leonard comes home. And it wants but three days—three short, short days, and we shall see him again, and all will go well with us once more."

The Captain said nothing, but in his sad face I saw that he sorrowed for me, and in his grave eyes I read the warning which did not leave his lips.

CHAPTER VIII.

THE DAY BEFORE.

THEY were very patient with me, the Captain and Celia, while the madness was in my blood. They let me talk as wildly as I pleased, and did not argue. But on the third day Celia put her foot down.

"I will hear nothing more, Laddy," she said. "You have spent three days in dreams of blood-shed and battle. Talk to me about your mother, if you please. I shall never tire of looking at her eyes. They are like yours—when you do not madden yourself with the recollection of that story. Let us picture the sweet life in the Polish village with the chateau beside it, and the girls dancing. Let us play their waltz, or let us go up to the wall and talk of Leonard. But no more battles."

It was a wise prohibition, and I had to obey. My thoughts were directed into a new channel, and the furies which had taken possession of me were, for the moment at least, expelled.

Four days, then, to the twenty-first. Four long, tedious days.

Then three.

Then the days became hours, and at last we were only a single day—only four-and-twenty hours from the fixed time when Leonard should come back to us. "In riches or in poverty"—somehow, in spite of all obstacles—he was to return to Celia's Arbour on the evening of the twenty-first of June, 1858. How would he come back, and what would be his history?

"If he is changed Laddy," said Celia, "he will find us changed too. You, poor boy, under a promise to go out and get killed for Poland. Not that you shall go in spite of the old patriot. And I—what am I, Laddy?"

"You are like Andromeda chained to the rock, waiting for the monster to come and devour her.

Or you are like an Athenian maiden going out to the youth-devouring Minotaur. But patience; Perseus came to Andromeda, and Theseus killed the Minotaur. I fancy the Minotaur must have been a tall and rather imposing animal to look at, six feet high at least, with a heavy white moustache and a military carriage. And very likely he wore blue spectacles out of doors."

"And what was Theseus like?"

"I think we will call him Perseus, and our monster shall be Andromeda's terror. There is an ugly story, you know, about Theseus and Ariadne."

Cis flushed a sweet rosy red.

"Then tell me what Perseus was like."

"He was about as tall as the monster, perhaps not quite. He was very handsome, had curly brown hair, perhaps he had a moustache, he was about four-and-twenty years of age; he was greatly esteemed by everybody because he was so brave and strong; there was a mystery about his birth which only made him more romantic; there was, you know, about a good many of the ancients. Theseus, for instance, Achilles, Œdipus—the damsels all fell in love with him because there was no one in all Greece or the Isles half so handsome; but he kept himself away from all of them; I believe there is a story about some Queen offering him half her throne if he would marry her, but he would not—declined in the most respectful, but unmistakable terms. When she received his answer, and sent half-a-dozen men to murder him—because terrible is the wrath of a woman whose beauty has been despised—he stood with his back against a wall, with his short sword held so, and with his shield held in the other hand, he made mincemeat of all those six murderers together, and went on his way without further molestation. There was a Dryad once, too, who met him in an Arcadian forest, and proffered him, in return for his love, half the balance of her life. She said she didn't know how much there was left to run, but she thought about fifteen hundred years or so, when she and her sister, and the great God Pan, would all be snuffed out together. Perseus told her that Love was immortal, and not a slave to be bought or sold. So he passed away, and the Dryad, sitting under a tree, slowly pined and pined till Orpheus found her at last changed into the strings of an

Æolian harp, and sighing most melodiously when the western breeze blew upon it. Perseus——"

"Laddy, talk sense."

"I can't, Cis. I feel as if Leonard was coming home to lift a great weight from both our hearts. I do not know how. I feel it. Perseus, however, was not callous to female loveliness, only he had given his heart away five years before, Cis, five years before."

"Laddy, I forbid you to go on."

"It is not a made-up story, Cis. I am certain it is all true. Arthur and Barbarossa are coming some day, to remove the miseries of the people. Why not Leonard to take away our troubles? We had no troubles when he went away. Now we are hampered and fettered, by no fault of our own, and I see no way out of it."

"Does the Captain know that it is so near?"

"Yes, he has not spoken of it to me, and he will not, I am sure. But he knows, and is looking forward. Last night I heard his step for an hour in his room, after he had gone to bed. He was thinking of Leonard, and could not sleep. And this morning he told Mrs. Jeram that you were going to stay all night to-morrow."

"Did he? The kind old Captain!"

"And that there would be another guest, and she was to get supper, a magnificent supper. The other guest, he explained, was to have his own room, and you were to have the spare room. Then I interposed, and said that a better arrangement would be to put the stranger into the spare bed in my room, so that he would not have to turn out. He grumbled and laughed, but he gave way."

"So he knows—but no one else."

"No one else: not even poor old Mrs. Jeram."

"We have gained a little time," said Celia, "Herr Räumer has not asked yet for my decision; but he has not given me up; and I am sure he will not. My father says nothing; but he starts if I come upon him suddenly. How will Leonard be able to help us with him?"

How indeed? And yet, somehow he was going to help. I was quite sure of it.

"And how will Leonard help us?" I asked.

"It is no use hoping," said Celia. "Leonard can help neither of us."

"He will help you, somehow, Cis. Of that be very sure. But he cannot help me."

"He *shall* help you, Laddy. Do you think we are going to let you go off to be killed?"

"I must," I said. "I have partly got over the revengeful madness which filled my soul when Wassielewski told me my story; I can think of a Russian, now, without wanting to tear his heart out. But the old man is right, I owe my life to the same cause in which my father and my mother lost theirs. If I can do anything for Poland, I must. And if Wassielewski tells me that it will be good for my country if I go out to get shot in his name, why I must do that. And I have sworn to do it on the cross that my father carved."

"Sworn! Laddy, of what power is an oath made under those conditions? You were maddened when you swore that oath. That old enthusiast ought never to have told you the story."

"Cis, dear. If I were to break that oath, it would break his heart. There is no way out of it at all. I *must* go."

That was the real reason. Heaven knows that during the first transport of rage, while before my eyes moved, visible in all the details, the long line of carts full of children, escorted by cavalry, and followed by shrieking women, running blindly along in the snow, and among them my poor mother there was no scheme of vengeance, however mad, into which I wouldn't have plunged with joy. With calmer thoughts came better judgment, and I hope I shall not be accused of insensibility because I listened to Celia when she said that the perils of hopeless insurrection were not what my mother's death called for. There is no blacker story in all the black record of Russia than that robbery and murder of those helpless children; no wail yet resounding within the vaults of space than my poor mother's last cry for her stolen child. And yet, O sweet pure eyes; O tender face; O lips of soft and compassionate mould—would you wish in return for your death another tale of misery and retribution?

And if I did not go when the old man should think it the time to summon me, I should break his heart. It was the dream of his old age to carry back with him the son of his murdered mistress. He thought that because his own life had been spent in brooding over that cruel crime all good

Poles at home had done the same thing, and he dreamed that he had but to show himself with me beside him to say, "This is the child of Roman Pulaski, tortured to death in the mines, and Claudia who died of cold and fatigue trying to save the child," and that thousands would rise from all quarters to die for Poland. For at least *he* entertained no illusions of possible success. Poland could not free herself in his lifetime; of that he was quite certain. All the more honour to those who, knowing the worst, were ready to brave the inevitable.

When a man fixes his thoughts incessantly upon one thing, when day and night he is always dwelling upon a great aim, there comes or seems to come unto him, when his mind is charged with figures of the present and the future, the gift of prophecy. The mist which falls upon the spirit of the Highland seer is gloomy always, and full of woe. The prophet is always like him who would prophecy no good concerning Ahab, but only evil. As for me, I think:

> "Too dearly would be won
> The prescience of another's pain,
> If purchased by mine own."

Six years ago, when the maddest of all modern revolts, that of the Commune of Paris, was staggering to its doom in blood and flame, there was one man among the leaders, Delescluze by name, who out of a life of over sixty years had spent between thirty and forty in prison, for the sacred cause of the people. Twice had he travelled backwards and forwards on that cruel and stifling voyage between Brest and Cayenne. Many times had he been arrested on suspicion, he had been hauled before judges, brow-beaten, scoffed and punished; had he been in Prussia he would have had the administration of stick, with those cuffs, boxes of the ear, kicks, and addresses in the third person, which illustrate the superior sweetness and light of the land of *Geist*. Had he been in Russia he would have had the knout. As he was in France he only got prison, with insufficient food, and wretched lodging. There came the time of the Commune, prophesied by Heine, after the siege, when Delescluze for the first time in his life got his chance. It was really only the ghost of a chance, but he did his best with it. Of course he failed, as we know, and became, together with his party, a byword of execration, by him quite undeserved. When it was apparent, even to him, the most fervent believer in the Commune, that there really was no longer any hope left, the poor old man was sent forth to meet Death. He would not wait to be brought before a Court-martial, to have more questions to answer, more witnesses to hear examined, to listen to more speeches, to wait in suspense for the sentence which would do him to death, to go back to a miserable prison, and sit there till the hour struck, when in the cold grey of the spring dawn he was to be placed with his back against the wall of La Roquette and receive the bullets of the soldiers. All this was too wearisome. But he had to die. His work in the world was over. He had striven for the best; he had maintained his own ideal of purity and singleness of purpose; as he had lived for the Cause, so he would die amid its dying struggles. He descended into the street, took off his hat, as one should in the presence of Death, of God, and of the Judgment, and walked without a word along the way till he came to the first barricade. Up to this he climbed, and then standing, his long white hair streaming in the wind, his sorrowful eyes looking upwards, his face full of that great love for humanity which made him half divine, he awaited the bullet, which was not long in coming.

When I read the story of the death of Delescluze, when I conversed with a man who actually saw it, I thought of poor old Wassielewski, for such was he, as unselfish, as simple, as strong in his conviction, and careless of himself, if, by spending and being spent, he could advance the Cause.

With brave words and a great pretence at cheerfulness I comforted poor Celia, and prophesied her release; but I could not feel the assurance I pretended. How could Leonard, if he were ever so successful, free her so as to leave her father safe from the German's revenge? How could he release me from the oath which bound me to the old Pole, and yet not darken the last years of his life with the thought that the child of the Lady Claudia was a traitor to his mother's cause?

We had been living in a fool's paradise, expecting such great things; and now at the very time when they ought to be coming off, we were face to face with the cold truth.

"We must not think of ourselves any more, Laddy," said Cis, as if reading my heart. "If Leonard can help us, he will. At all events, he will be on our side. I shall wait patiently until I am called upon to give my answer, and then, Laddy—and then—if for my father's sake"—she broke off and left the sentence unfinished. "You must both of you try not to think badly of me."

"We shall never think badly of you, whatever you do, Cis," I said, a little huskily.

"Come home with me, Laddy," she said, rising from the grass. "It is nearly eight o'clock. See, the tide is high; we shall have everything to-morrow evening just as it was five years ago; a splendid evening; a flowing tide; the light of a midsummer sunset on the water; the buttercups and daisies out upon the meadow; the long green grass waving on the ramparts and grown up before the mouth of the cavern; you and I, dear Laddy, standing by the old gun, waiting for him. What was it he promised? 'In velvet or in rags—in riches or poverty, I will come to see you on the 21st of June, 1858.' And now it is the 20th. Laddy—tell me how he will come."

"We shall see him first," I said, "crossing the meadow, just down there. We shall know him by the backward toss of his head. Presently we shall see his brown curls, and then his eyes and his mouth. He will see us then, and his lips and eyes will laugh a welcome before he runs up the slope. Then he will spring upon us in his old way, and—and—where he said good-bye, Cis, he kissed you."

"We are older now," said Cis. "And do not be silly, sir. As if men want to kiss like children!"

"It depends, my dear," I replied wisely, "on the object. However, that will be the manner of his return. And then we shall all three march off to the Captain's, Leonard between us; and should be singing as we went, but for the look of the thing; Leonard will be asking us questions about the dear old Captain and everybody—wait—Cis—wait for four-and-twenty hours."

I went home with her. Herr Räumer was talking to Mrs. Tyrrell in the drawing-room. We had a little music. The German played and sang one or two of his Volkslieder in his most sentimental manner, but we listened very little. Mr. Tyrrell was in his office, and I crept down to see him.

He was sitting in an attitude of profound melancholy before a pile of papers.

"Shut the door, Laddy, boy," he said wearily. "Who is upstairs?"

'Herr Räumer, Mrs. Tyrrell, and Cis."

He sighed.

"He is beginning to worry about an answer. What would Celia say?"

"Celia would be made wretched for life. It cannot be. Is it quite, quite necessary?"

"There is one way out of it," he murmured.

I stood still and looked at him.

"What is the one way out of it?"

"There are two ways—Death and Dishonour. Let no one know, Laddy. Think of me as you must, only think that for no other cause would I ask this thing of my child. Poor Celia! Poor Celia!"

He drew his hand across his forehead.

"I cannot sleep—I cannot work—I can think of nothing else. Do you believe I *like* to have that man here—that cold and selfish cynic—that I willingly tolerate him in my house, to say nothing of seeing him hang about my daughter? But I am a lost man, Ladislas. I am a lost and guilty man, and I must abide my lot."

A lost and guilty man! And this the most successful man in the town!

He pointed to the safe painted outside "Herr Räumer."

"The papers are there—locked up. If I only had the key for one minute Celia would be free."

CHAPTER IX.

THE TWENTY-FIRST OF JUNE.

THE day fulfilled its promise of the evening: it was one of those most perfect and glorious days which sometimes fall in June, and make that month, in full summer and yet with all the hope and promise of the year before it, the most delightful of any. I rose early, because I could not sleep; but I found the Captain up before me, at work in the garden. But he prodded the ground nervously, and made little progress. At prayers he opened the Bible at random, and read what fell first before his eyes. It was a chapter of the Song of Solomon, and as he read his voice faltered.

"'The watchmen that go about the city found

me: to whom I said, Saw ye him whom my soul loveth?

"'It was but a little that I passed from them, but I found him whom my soul loveth?'"

Then he stopped, having read only the first four verses of the chapter; and to him, as to me, they seemed to be of good omen.

He did not mention Leonard's name, but he presently went upstairs, and I knew he was gone to see that the room was in order for him. He brought out certain articles of family plate which only saw the light on grand occasions: and I caught him making extensive and costly preparations with a couple of bottles of champagne. All day he was very serious. Nor did he, as usual, go out upon those mysterious rounds of his, of which I have spoken.

"Celia will come here to dinner, sir."

"Ay—ay—— The earlier the better. Celia cannot come too early or too often." He sat down in his wooden arm-chair and began to nurse his leg in a meditative fashion.

"Laddy——Celia Tyrrell is a very beautiful girl."

"Have you only found that out to-day, sir?" I asked. "Why, she is the most beautiful girl in all the world, I believe."

"I was thinking—Laddy—if things are all right—and they must be all right, or else he would have written—when he comes home—he might—I know I should have done so at his age—he might—fall in love with her. She must have a good husband, the best husband that we can find for her. Look high or low, Laddy, I can see no one but Leonard that will do for her."

"But you have not seen him yet. And he may have fallen in love with some one else."

"Nonsense, boy. As if I did not *know* what he is like. Curs don't grow out of lions' cubs; you can't turn a white boy into a nigger; and a Portugee, as every sailor knows, is a Portugee by birth."

Then we began, as we had done the night before, speculating how the wanderer would return. He was above all things, according to the Captain, to be strong, handsome, and successful.

Celia came to our mid-day dinner, and when it was over we moved into the garden, and sat under the old mulberry tree. The sun was streaming full upon the sheet of water before us, and a light breeze crisped the surface.

We spread rugs on the grass, and all three sat down upon them, Celia lying with her head on the Captain's knees, while he sat with his back against the tree. It was peaceful and quiet, save for the boom of the mill hard by, and to that we were accustomed.

The excitement of the day touched Celia's cheek with a light flush, and heightened the brightness of her eyes. I had never before seen her more perfectly beautiful than on that afternoon. The Captain's eyes rested on her face, and his hand was in her hair with a gentle caress.

"This was where you were sleeping," she said in a low voice, "when he first came."

We did not say "Leonard" on this day, because all our minds were full of him, and a pronoun was quite as useful as the noun.

The Captain nodded his head.

"Just here, my dear," he replied, "and just such an afternoon as this, without the breeze, and may be a thought warmer. It was in August, when the mulberries are ripe. I came out after dinner. My dinners were solitary enough then, before I had the boys to mess with me, and I sat under the tree and smoked my pipe. Then I fell fast asleep. What woke me was the mulberries dropping on my face, and then I looked up and saw the pretty rogue laughing at me, with his mouth full of mulberries, and his face and hands stained black with mulberry juice. Ho! ho! and he began to laugh at once. What a boy he was! What a boy! Never any boy like him for spirit. A thousand pities he wasn't a sailor."

"And you never lost sight of him after that?" said Celia.

"No, my pretty—never after that. It was a matter of a year or two though before I found out that I was a lonely old bachelor, and wanted the boys with me. Wanted them badly, you may be sure. We had a good spell of fine weather, those years you were both of you at school, Laddy, hadn't we?"

"Indeed we had, sir."

"I was at sea when I was thirteen, and I hadn't much experience of shore-going boys till then. To be sure, I was always fond of watching boys at play, and talking to them—perhaps throwing in a word on the great subject of duty. But Lord! the things I learned from those two! The pretty ways of them when they were next door to babies! and their growing up to be boys together bit by bit. Then how they grew to be self-reliant, and how we all grew to understand each other! My dear," the good old man continued simply, 'if I were to give you what is best for all of us, man or woman, I would give you children. You can't distrust the Lord when you have felt what it is for the little children to trust and love you. I never had a wife, but I have had two boys all the same. Both good sons to me—Laddy, there, will not be jealous—and to each his gifts; but Leonard was born, like Nelson, without fear."

"Always a brave boy, was he not, Captain?" Celia murmured.

"It's a rare gift. Most of us learn by experience how to go into action without fear, and a fight is a red-letter day for soldiers as well as sailors. But Leonard would have gone in laughing as a middy. It's a beautiful thing to see a plucky boy! You remember how he used to come home after a fight, Laddy? The other boy always struck his colours, eh?—and generous and thoughtful with it, too. Why did I ever consent to his going away for five years?"

"Patience!" said Cis. "Tell me more about him."

We kept the Captain amused all the afternoon with yarns of Leonard's school life, while in the quiet garden, the big bumble bees droned, and the hollyhocks turned their great foolish faces to the sun, while the mill went grinding as the water ran out with the tide to the deep-toned music of its heavily-turning wheels, and the golden sunshine of June lay upon the rippled waters of the mill-dam, and lit with flashes of dazzling light the leaves of the trees upon the little island redoubt.

At six I brought out a table and chair, and we had tea in the garden, also under the mulberry tree. Cis made it for us; she always made it so much better than we did.

And then the time began to drag, and the Captain to look at his watch furtively. Presently the mill stopped, and everything became quite still. That meant that it was seven o'clock.

Then Celia and I rose from the table.

"We are going for a walk, Captain," said Cis.

"Mayn't I go too?" he asked wistfully.

She shook her head with decision.

"Certainly not. You have got to stay at home. We have got to go to the walls and—and walk about there—and talk. And we shall not be back till a quarter to nine, or perhaps later. Perhaps, Captain, we shall bring you some news—Oh! what news will it be?" she cried eagerly.

No one on the Queen's Bastion, when we got there; Celia's Arbour as deserted as any outwork of Palmyra; no one on the long straight stretch of wall between the gate and the Bastion—not even a nurse with children; and our own corner as green and grassy, as shaded by the great elm, as when, five years ago, Leonard bade us farewell there. Nothing changed here, at any rate.

"Laddy," whispered Celia, in awe-struck tones, "suppose, after all, he should not come."

"He will come, Celia; but we are an hour before our time."

"Oh! what a long day it has been! I am selfish. I have been able to think of nothing but my own troubles until to-day. And now they seem to be all forgotten in this great anxiety."

We walk up and down the quiet wall, talking idly of things unimportant, talking to pass the time.

Eight struck from half-a-dozen clocks, from the clock in the Dockyard, the clock on the Ordnance Wharf, the clock of St. Faith's, the clock of St. John's, from all of them. The splendid sun was sloping fast towards Jack the Painter's Point; the great harbour, for it was high tide, just as on that night when Leonard went away, was a vast lake of molten fire, with sapphire edging below our feet. We leaned against the rampart, and looked out, but we were no longer thinking of the Harbour or the light upon it.

Five years, since he left us, a tall stripling of seventeen, to seek his fortune in the wide and friendless world. Five years. Celia was a little girl who was now so tall and fair. In her, at least, Leonard would not be disappointed. And I? Well, I suppose I was much the same to look at. And for my fortunes, there was little to tell, and nothing to be proud of. Only a music-master in a provincial town; only an organist to a church; a composer of simple songs to please myself and Celia. But what would he be like? What tale would he have to tell us? What adventures to relate? In what part of the world had his fortunes drifted him?

Five years. They make a girl into a woman; a boy into a man; five links in the chain of time; time to make new friends, to form and lose new loves; to strengthen a purpose; to make or mar a life. Had they made, or had they marred, the life of Leonard?

"What will he say when he sees us?" murmured Celia.

"He will remember, Cis, the words of Spenser—

"'Tell me, ye merchants' daughters, did ye see
So fair a creature in your town before?
So sweet, so lovely, and so mild as she,
Adorned with beauty's grace and virtue's store.'"

"Don't, Laddy, please. Let us talk only of him until he comes."

"Where is he now?" she whispered, looking round. "On the road walking quickly, so as to keep his promise to the minute? Is he in the train? Do you think he came last night, and has been hiding away in an hotel all day for fear of meeting us before the time? Oh, Laddy, let us move about at least. I cannot stand here doing nothing."

The minutes passed slowly on. I looked at my watch.

"Twenty minutes more. Courage, Cis! Only twenty minutes. Where are your thoughts now?"

"I was thinking of the dear old time. Listening to his talk about the great world—it lay over there, you remember, behind the harbour and the hill. Wishing I had been a man, to go with him and fight the world beside him."

"Five years ago, Cis! Why, Leonard may have lost his faith in his own power, and——"

"Don't, Laddy. Not now. It is all we have to believe in. And—and—Laddy—please—do not tell him what you told me."

"I understand, dear Cis. I have forgotten that I ever told you."

"Not but that you made me happy—happy and proud; any girl would be proud to think of having had, if only for a day, such a hope and such a love.

But he must never know. And yet I should be ashamed to hide things from him."

"Until you tell him yourself then, Cis."

I looked at my watch again. Heavens! had Time tumbled down and hurt himself, so that he could only crawl? Only a quarter-past eight. Fifteen minutes more.

"Where are you now, Cis?"

"I am thinking what a difference he will see in us, and we in him. Why, I was only a child, a girl of fourteen, then, and you were only fifteen."

"At least," I said, "he will see no difference in me. I am no taller and no straighter. But you—oh! Celia, if you only knew how beautiful he will think you!"

"That is only what you think, dear Laddy. Beautiful? Oh! if I ever have any thoughts that are not common or mean, it is because you have put them into my heart. What should I be now, if I had not had you, all these five long years?"

She stooped, and kissed my cheek.

I could endure that now—I could kiss her in return—without that old passionate yearning which, a very little while before, had been wont to set the blood tingling in every pulse at very sight of her.

The monks of old were quite right in one thing, though as a Protestant I am bound to think that they had a very confused and imperfect sort of perception. I mean that you may, by dint of resolution and patience—they would call it prayer and penance—quite beat down and entirely subdue any inclination of the heart or intellect. They started with the supposition that every man was bound to fall in love with every woman. That is absurd, but an intelligible position on the score of monkish ignorance. I, for my part, was only in danger once of falling in love. Having seen, known, and learned the sweet nature of one woman, it was not possible that I should ever fall in love with another.

We kissed each other on the lips, and then we sat with clasped hands upon the sloping bank, waiting. At last the clock struck the half-hour, and we turned together and looked across the green.

Suddenly came a figure, a ragged figure, walking swiftly across the grass.

Yes, as I had prophesied, by the backward fling of his head, by the proud carriage, by the firm and elastic walk, we knew him.

Celia clasped my hands convulsively, and I hers; and before she sprang to her feet she whispered :

"See, he is ragged—he is poor—he has failed. Not a word, not a look, Laddy, to let him see what we feel. Oh, my poor Leonard! my poor Leonard!"

She made a little moan, and then ran forward to meet him. For it was Leonard himself and no other who, at sight of us, came bounding up the grass slope with quick and eager step, and in a moment was with us, holding Celia by both his hands, and gazing in her face with eyes that spoke of love—of love—of love. Who could mistake that look! Not Celia, who met the look once, and then dropped her eyes shamefaced. Not I, who knew by sad experience what love might be, how strong a king, how great a conqueror.

In one glance we caught the melancholy truth. He was in rags; there was no petty pretence of genteel shabbiness; there was no half failure, he was in rags absolute. He wore a battered old felt hat, the brim of which, partly torn, hung over his right eye; he had on a coat which was a miracle for shabbiness; it was green where it ought to have been black; shiny where it had once exhibited a youthful gloss; and it had a great hole on the left shoulder, such a hole as would be caused by carrying a bundle on a stick. The coat, an old frock, was fastened by the two surviving buttons across his chest. One could see that he had no waistcoat, and his trousers were in the last stage of dilapidation and decay. He wore neither collar nor necktie. But it was Leonard. There was no mistake about him. Leonard come back to us on the day that he promised. Leonard, dressed as a beggar, and stepping like a prince.

"Celia!—Laddy!"

"Leonard!"

Both hands; not one. And as he clasped her tight she drew nearer to him, and like a child who holds up his face to be kissed, she looked up at him. But there was no kiss. Men, as Celia said, are not like children, always wanting to kiss. Oho! Cis, as if you knew! Man's love is like the morning sun, which, falling on his bride, the earth, draws up sweet mists which rise to hide her blushes. Leonard was come back, and now I understood how in her mind Leonard was to make all straight, because

Leonard loved her, and she loved Leonard. And he a beggar.

He got one hand free, and gave it to me.

"Laddy! Well? You at least are not changed. But look at Celia!"

"Take off your hat, Leonard," she said. "Let us look at your face. Laddy! He is just the same, except for that." She laughed, and patted her own upper lip with her fingers. Leonard had grown a great moustache. "And his face is bronzed. Where have you been, sir, to get your face so brown? Fie! what a bad hat! A great hole in the side of it, and look what a coat to come home in! Dear, dear, before we take him home to the Captain we must dress him up. What a pity he is too tall to wear your things, Laddy. Now we have found him again we will never let him go. Will we? He is our prodigal son, Laddy, who has come back to us—back to us," and here she broke down, and burst into tears. "We have so longed for you, have we not, Laddy? And the time has been so weary, waiting for you."

"But I am come at last, Celia," he said, with eyes that filled—I had never before seen a tear in

Leonard's eyes—"I have kept my promise. See—in rags and tatters, with empty pockets." He turned them out.

"What does it matter," she cried, "so long as we have you, how you come?"

"And the Captain?"

"He is well," I told him, "and waiting at home for us all. Come, Leonard."

He hesitated, and looked with a humorous smile at his ragged habiliments.

"What will the Captain say to these rags? Dear old boy, it is not as he expects, is it? Nor as you expected, Celia."

"No, Leonard, I am sorry for your ill-success. But it wasn't your own fault?"

"No, certainly not my own fault," he replied, with a queer look. "Not my own fault. I have done my best. Celia and Laddy! How jolly it is to say the two names over again with their owners in the old place! And how often have I said them to myself, thousands of miles away,"—he had been a traveller, then. "Suppose you two go first to the Captain, and prepare him. Will not that be best? Say that he must not be surprised to find me coming home in a sad plight—all in rags, you know—tell him about the hat, Laddy, and then—I will only be a quarter of an hour after you—he won't be so very much shocked. Will you do this? Good. Then, in a quarter of an hour, I will be there."

He caught Celia's hand and kissed it, looking her in the eyes half lovingly, half amused, and ran down the slope as lightly as if he was come back a conquering prince.

We looked at each other in stupefaction. Was it really Leonard? Was it a strange dream?

"Can you understand it, Celia?"

"Not yet, Laddy, dear. Do not speak to me just now."

"His hands were white," I went on, unheeding, "like the hands of a gentleman; his boots were good and new, the boots of a gentleman; and his face—did that look like the face of a beggar, Celia?"

"Always the same face, Laddy. The dearest face in all the world to you and to me, isn't it? Poor and in rags. Poor—poor Leonard!"

"I don't know," I replied, "whether your face isn't dearer to me than Leonard's. That is because

I have seen more of it, perhaps. But why is he in such a dreadful plight? He said he had been thousands of miles away. He must have been an emigrant in America, and failed."

Of course that was it. He must have gone to America as an emigrant and failed.

We crept slowly and sadly back, like a pair of guilty children. What were we to say to the Captain? Who should break the news?

CHAPTER X.

"A SURPRISE."

THE Captain, dressed in his Sunday blue uniform coat and white ducks, was sitting at his table, pretending to read. At least he had a book open before him, but I observed that it was upside down, and it was not usual with the Captain to read with the book in that position. But it was getting dark; the sunset gun had gone half an hour before; and the twilight of the longest day was lying over the garden and the smooth waters of the Mill Dam. Perhaps, therefore, the Captain could see to read no more, and, indeed, his eyes were not so good as they had been. The candles were on the table, but they were not lit; and the cloth was laid for supper. He had been listening to our footsteps, and when we came in looked up with a quick air of expectation which changed to disappointment.

"You two?" he cried. "Back again?—And alone—alone?"

We had pretended, all day long, not to know who was coming in the evening, but the pretence broke down now.

Celia threw her arms round his neck and kissed him.

"Dear old Captain," she whispered; "yes, he has come back—our Leonard has come home again to us."

He started to his feet trembling.

"Where is he, then? Why do you look at me like that? Why does he not come to me? What is it, Laddy?"

"Perhaps, sir, he is ashamed to come."

"Ashamed? Leonard ashamed? Why?"

"Suppose," said Celia, laying her hand on the Captain's shoulder, "suppose, Captain dear, that our boy, after he had promised his friends to come back triumphant, found the world too strong for him, and had to come back—in poverty, and not triumphant at all?"

"Is that all?" cried the stout old Captain. "Leonard has failed, has he? That is nothing. Many a lad fails at first. Give him rope enough and no favour, and he'll do in the long-run. It's the confounded favour plays the mischief, ashore as well as afloat. Leonard has not had fair play. Where is the boy?"

And at this moment a step in the hall, and a scream, and a shuffle, showed that the "boy" was arrived, and in the arms of the faithful Jeram.

"Oh, my beautiful boy—oh! my bonnie boy. Let your old nurse kiss you once again—and you so tall and brave."

The Captain could restrain himself no longer.

"Leonard," he shouted, breaking through Celia's arms, "Leonard, ahoy! Welcome home, my lad."

We caught each other's hands and trembled, waiting for the moment when the Captain should discover the rags and tatters.

"Shall I light the candles, Laddy?"

"Not yet, Celia. Yes—do—it will be best so. The Captain must know all in a few minutes."

They were in the hall, laughing, shaking hands,

and asking each other all round, and all at once, how they were, and how they had been.

"Supper at once, Mrs. Jeram," cried the jolly old Captain. "Supper at once. Such a feast we will make. And none of your fanteegs about not sitting down with Miss Celia, Mrs. Jeram, if you please. Now then, Leonard, my boy, come and talk to Laddy and Celia. Lord! how glad I am, how glad I am!"

We looked at each other. One moment, and the rags would be visible to the naked eye.

"Poor Leonard—Oh, poor Leonard!" Celia whispered.

Then we started and cried out together, for the Captain and he came in together, the Captain, with his hand upon Leonard's stalwart shoulder, and a face which was like the ocean for its multitudinous smile.

But where were the rags?

They were gone. Before us stood the handsomest man, I believe, in all the world. He was nearly six feet high, his light brown hair lay in short crisp curls upon his head, his eyes had the frankest, loyalest look in them that I have ever seen in any man, and at that moment the happiest look as well. I declare that I have never seen in all my forty years of life so splendid a man as Leonard was at five-and-twenty. As he did not look one-half so splendid in rags one is bound to admit that clothes do improve even the finest figure. And as he stood in the doorway with the Captain I was dazzled by the beauty and vigour of the man. As for his dress, it was nothing but a plain black coat, with light summer trousers, just as any gentleman might wear. That was it: any *gentleman.*

He had succeeded, then.

"I beg your pardon, Celia, and yours, Laddy," said Leonard. "The foolish thought came into my head to see how you would receive me if I were to return in poverty and rags. So I masqueraded. I meant to come on here and see the Captain, too, just as I was. But I had not the heart when I saw the pain it gave you. So I made an excuse and gave up the silly trick. Forgive me Celia."

Her eyes, which had been frank with pity, looked more shyly into Leonard's as she listened.

"What is there to forgive Leonard? If we were glad to have you back again any way, how much more glad ought we to be that you have come back —as you are?"

"But you do not know me—as I am."

"Come, come, no explanations now," cried the Captain. "Supper first, talk afterwards. I am so glad. Here's something I found to-day in your room, Master Leonard. See if you have forgotten the old tune."

Of course he had not forgotten it. It was the old fife on which he used to play the "Roast Beef of Old England" every Sunday before dinner. Leonard laughed, took up his position at the door, and piped lustily while the maid brought in the supper.

We all sat down, I at the end, and Celia on the Captain's right, Leonard at his left, and Mrs. Jeram next him. I don't think we ate much at that supper, though it consisted of cold fowls and ham, the Captain's fixed idea of what a supper ought to be, but we had a bottle of champagne, a drink looked upon in those days as a costly luxury, to be reserved for weddings, Christmas dinners, and such great occasions. What greater occasion than the welcome home of the exile!

"No explanations till after supper," repeated the Captain. "Celia, my pretty, not a question. Take another wing, my dear. No? Then Leonard shall have it. Leonard, my boy, here's to you again. Your health, my lad. After supper you shall tell us all. I am so glad."

Supper finished, I began.

"Now, Leonard."

"Not yet," said the Captain. "The Bible and Prayer-book, Laddy, my boy."

Putting on his glasses, the old man turned over the pages till he found what he wanted.

Then he laid his hand upon the place and looked up.

"Before I read the chapter," he said, "I wish to say that I thank God for my two boys, and for the trust that has always been with me, firm and strong, that the one who was away in the world would turn out as good in the matter of duty as the one who stayed with me."

And then, to our extreme discomfiture, he proceeded to read the story of the Prodigal Son. What on earth had the Prodigal Son to do with us at this juncture? Prayers despatched—he was always brief, after the manner of sailors, over prayers—he made another little speech.

"Since Leonard went away," he said, "which is five years to-day, as long a cruise as ever I made in the old days, I've been drawn towards this parable till I know it by heart. I've thought at times—What if Leonard were to come back like that young man with five years' neglect of duty upon his mind! How should we have to receive him? And here I find the directions laid down plain. Lord! Lord! how plain a man's course is marked out for him, with lighthouses along the coast, and the mariner's compass, and the stars to steer by at night—if only he would use his eyes. Well, Mrs. Jeram, ma'am, and Celia, and Laddy, it was clear what we all had to do. And though a dreadful thought crossed my mind when you came home without him, and beat about the bush, talking of failure and such things, which I now perceive to have been only the remains of the devilment that always hung about the lad, I went out into the passage bold, and prepared, I hope, to act according to open orders. Somehow, we generally think, when we read this Divine parable, of the young man.

To-night, all through supper, I've been thinking about his father, and I have been pitying that father. What if his boy, who had been away from home for five years or thereabouts, came home to him, not as he did, in rags and disgrace, but proud and tall, bringing his sheaves with him, my dear—bringing his sheaves with him! Think of that; for I am so glad, Leonard, I am so glad and happy."

We were all silent while the good old man cleared his throat and wiped his eyes. Celia leaned her head upon his shoulder and wept unrestrainedly.

"Therefore I say," continued the Captain, "the Lord be thanked for all His mercies, and if Laddy will play the Hundredth Psalm, and Celia will sing it with him, I think it would do good both to Mrs. Jeram and to me."

"Thank you, my children," he said, when we had finished. "That hymn expresses my feelings exactly. And now, Leonard, that we've got the decks clear of all superfluous gear and are ship-shape, and have had supper, and drunk the champagne, and thanked God, I will light my pipe, and Celia shall mix me the customary—double ration to-night, my pretty—and you shall give us the log."

"Shall I begin at the end, sir, or at the beginning?" asked Leonard.

"The end," said Celia.

"The beginning," said the Captain, both in a breath.

"What do you say, Mrs. Jeram?" Leonard asked the old lady.

She said, crossing her hands before her, that, beginning or end, it would be all the same to her; that she was quite satisfied to see him back again, and the beautifullest boy he was that God ever made—flash o' lighting about the place just as he always had a done; and she was contented, so long as he was well and happy, to wait for that story for ever, so as she could only look at him.

"What do you say, Laddy?"

"Ask the Captain," I said. "He commands this ship, but Celia is our passenger."

"Good," said the Captain. "My dear, the ship's in luck to get such a lovely passenger as you. And you shall command the ship instead of me, so long as you don't run her ashore. Now then, Leonard, the end of the log first."

"First," said Leonard, "by way of preface to my log—you remember this?"

He drew a black ribbon from his neck with a gold ring upon it.

"A good beginning, my lad—your mother's ring."

"You remember what you said to me when you gave it to me? That it was an emblem of honour and purity among women, and that I was to wear it only so long as I could deserve it?"

"Ay—ay. This is a very good beginning of the end, Celia, my love. Go, on Leonard."

"I believe I have not forfeited the right to wear it still, sir."

"I never thought you would," said the Captain, with decision. "Go on, my lad,—keep on paying-out the line."

"Then the end is," he said modestly, "that I bear Her Majesty's Commission, and am a Captain in the Hundred and Twentieth. We disembarked from India a week ago, and are now lying in the Old Kent Barracks in this town. Here, sir, are my medals—Alma, Inkermann, Sebastopol, and India. I have seen service since I left you, and I have gone through all the fighting without a wound or a day's illness."

"You are a combatant officer in Her Majesty's

service like myself?" cried the Captain, springing to his feet.

"I am Captain Copleston, raised from the ranks by singular good fortune; and five years ago a raw recruit sitting on a wooden bench at Westminster, with all my work ahead."

"Like me, he has seen service; like me, he holds Her Majesty's Commission; like me, he can show his medals." He spread out his hands solemnly. "Children, children"—he spoke to Celia and to me—"did we ever dare to think of this?"

CHAPTER XI.

LEONARD TELLS HIS STORY.

THEN Leonard began his story. The room was lit by the single pair of candles standing one each side of the model of the *Asia* on the mantelshelf. The Captain sat with his pipe in his wooden chair, his honest red face glowing with satisfaction, and beside him Celia leaning on his shoulder and listening with rapt eyes. It was Dido listening to Æneas. "With varied talk did Dido prolong the night, deep were the draughts of love she drank. 'Come,' said she, 'my guest, and tell us from the first beginning the stratagems of the enemy and the hap of our country then, and your own wanderings, for this is now the *fifth* summer that carries you a wanderer o'er every land and sea.'" As Dido wept to hear, so did Celia sigh and sob and catch her breath as

Leonard told his story. No Gascon, he ; but there are stories in which the hero, be he as modest as a wood-nymph, needs must proclaim his heroism. And a hero at four-and-twenty is ten times as interesting as a hero of sixty.

> " O, talk not to me of a name great in story,
> The days of our youth are the days of our glory ;
> And the myrtle and ivy of sweet two-and-twenty
> Are worth all your laurels, though ever so plenty."

And what is it when the myrtle and ivy of two-and-twenty have real laurels mixed up with them ?

A philosopher so great that people grovel before his name, in a work on the Subjection of Women, makes the astounding statement that the influence of woman has always been in the direction of peace and the avoidance of war. Pity he had not read history by the light of poetry. Was there ever, one asks in astonishment, a time when women did not love courage and strength ? It was not only in the days of chivalry that young knights fought before the eyes of their mistresses—

> " Since doughty deeds my lady please,
> Right soon I'll mount my steed ;
> And strong his arm and fast his seat
> That bears frae me the meed."

How could it be otherwise? We love the qualities which most we lack. If women ceased to be gentle, tender, soft—what we call womanly—we should leave off falling in love. That is most certain. Who ever fell in love with one of the unsexed women? And I suppose if men ceased to be strong and courageous, women would leave off accepting and rejoicing in their love. Dido drank deep draughts of love listening to the tale of Æneas which was, as Scarron many years afterwards remarked, extremely long and rather dull. So sat Celia listening to a much more wonderful story of battle and endurance. Or, I thought, she was more like the gentle maid of Venice than the proud Phœnician queen. With such sweetness did Desdemona listen when the valiant Moor told of the dangers he had passed. Did she, as John Stuart Mill would have us believe, incline him to ways of peace? Quite the contrary; this sweet and gentle Desdemona wished "that Heaven had made her such a man," and when her lord must go to slay the Turk she would fain go with him. My gentle Celia wept over the brave soldiers who went forth to fight, and again over those who were brought home to die; but her heart, womanlike, was ready to open out to the most valiant.

"I went up to town," he began, "with my ten pounds, as you all know. When I arrived at Waterloo Station I discovered for the first time that I had formed no plans how to begin. The problem before me was the old difficulty, how a man with a reasonably good education and no friends had best start so as to become a gentleman. I faced that problem for a fortnight, trying to find a practical solution. I might become a clerk—and end there; a mechanical copying clerk in a City office!"

"Faugh!" said the Captain.

"Or an usher in a school—and end there."

"Fudge!" said the Captain.

"Or a strolling actor, and trust to chance to make a name for myself."

"Pshaw!" said the Captain.

"There were men, I knew, who made money by writing for the papers. I thought I might write too, and I found out where they mostly resorted, and tried to talk to them. But that profession, I very soon discovered, wanted other qualities than

I possessed. Laddy might have taken to writing; but it was not my gift."

"Right," said the Captain. "Laddy, you remember the story of my old messmate who once wrote a novel. 'Twas his ruin, poor fellow. Never lifted his head afterwards. Go on, Leonard."

"All the time I was looking about me the money, of course, was melting fast. I might have made it last longer, I dare say; but I was ignorant, and got cheated. One morning I awoke to the consciousness that there was nothing left at all except the purse. Well, sir, I declare that I was relieved. The problem was solved, because I knew then that the only line possible for me was to enlist. I went down to Westminster and took the shilling. Of course I was too proud to enlist under any but my own name. Going a soldiering is no disgrace."

"Right," said the Captain.

"Well," he went on, "it is no use pretending I was happy at first, because the life was hard, and the companionship was rough. But the drill came easy to me who had seen so many drills upon the Common, and, after a bit, I found myself as good a soldier as any of them. One fretted a little under the rules and the discipline; that was natural at first. There seemed too much pipeclay and too little personal ease. One or two of the sergeants were unfair on the men too, and bore little spites. Some of the officers were martinets; I offended one because I refused to become a servant."

"You a servant, Leonard!" cried Celia.

He laughed.

"The officers like a smart lad; but it was not to be a valet that I enlisted, and I refused, as a good many others refused. Our lads were mostly sturdy Lancashire boys, proud of being soldiers, but had not enlisted to black other men's boots. It makes me angry now—which is absurd—to think that I should have been asked to become a lackey. Well, it was a hard life, that in the ranks. Not the discipline, nor the work, nor the drill—though these were hard enough. It was the roughness of the men. There were one or two gentlemen among us—one fellow who had been an officer in the Rifles—but they were a bad and hopeless lot, who kept up as best they could the vices which had ruined them. They were worse than any of the rough rollicking countryside lads. I can't say I had much room for hope in those days, Celia."

She reddened, but said nothing. I remembered, suddenly, what he might mean.

"Things looked about as black for a few months as they well could. Rough work, rough food, rough campaigning. I thought of Coleridge and his adventures as a private, but *he* turned back, while I—for there was nothing else to do—resolved to keep on. And then, bit by bit, one got to like it. For one thing, I could do all sorts of things better than most men—my training with the Poles came in there—it was found that I could fence: it got about that I played cricket, and I was put in the eleven—to play in the matches of the regiment, officers and men together; once, when we had a little row with each other, it was found that I could handle my fists, which always gains a man respect. And then they came to call me Gentleman Jack; and, as I heard afterwards, the officers got to know it, and the Colonel kept his eye upon me. Of course one may wear the soldier's jacket very well without falling into any of the pits which are temptations to these poor fellows, so that it was easy enough getting the good conduct stripe, and to be even made corporal. The first proud day, however, was that when I was made a sergeant, with as good a knowledge of my work, I believe, as any sergeant in the Line."

Mrs. Jeram shook her head.

"More," she said, "much more."

"A sergeant," said Leonard. "It sounds so little now, but to me, then, it seemed so much. The first real step upwards out of the ruck. The old dream that I should return triumphant somehow was gone long since, or it was a dream that had no longer any faith belonging to it. And I began to say to myself that to win my way after two years to a sergeant's stripes was perhaps as much honour as Providence intended for me."

The Captain murmured something about mysterious ways. Then he patted Celia's head tenderly, and begged Leonard to keep on his course.

"Well," said Leonard, "you have heard how the great luck began. It was just before the Crimean War that I got the stripes. We were among the first regiments ordered. How well I remember embarking at this very place, half afraid, and half hoping, to see you all, but I did not."

"We were there, Leonard," said Celia, "when the first troops embarked. I think I remember them all going."

"It is a solemn thing," Leonard went on, "going off to war. It is not only that your life is to be hazarded—every man hazards his life in all sorts of ways as much as on a battlefield—but you feel that you are going to help in adding another chapter to the history of the world."

"Ay," said the Captain. "History means war."

"Let us pass over the first two or three months. We went to Varna, where we lost many men needlessly by cholera, waiting till the Generals could make up their minds. I suppose they could not avoid the delay, but it was a bad thing for the rank and file, and we were all right glad when the orders came to embark for the Crimea. We were amongst the earliest to land, and my first experience of fighting was at Alma. One gets used to the bullets after a bit; but the first time—you know, Captain——"

The Captain nodded.

"After Alma we might, as we know very well, have pushed straight on to Sebastopol. I doubt whether that would have finished the war, which had to be fought out somewhere. Russia had to learn that an immense army is not by itself proof of immense power. And so it was just as well, I believe, that we moved as we did.

"You know all about the battles—the Alma, Inkermann, Balaclava, and the rest. Our fellows went through most of the fighting, and, of course, I with the rest. The hardest day was Inkermann. We had just come in at daybreak from the trenches, where we had been on duty for four-and-twenty hours, when we were turned out to fight in the fog and rain. We fought in our greatcoats—well—all that is history. But the days of battle were red-letter days for all of us, and what tried us most was the inaction, and the dreary waiting work in the trenches. And yet it was that work which got me my commission.

"You know what it was we had to do. Before the Redan and the Malakoff were our batteries, the French attack on the Mamelon and the Malakoff was on our right. Separating our right from our left attack was the valley which they called the Valley of the Shadow of Death, along which they carried the wounded, and where the Russian shells, which went over the Twenty-one Gun Battery, fell and rolled till the place was literally paved with shells. It was a dangerous way by which to carry wounded men, and at night the troops went down by the Woronzow Road. It was easy work comparatively in the battery; you could see the shells flying over, and long before they fell you had plenty of time to dodge behind the next traverse: after a while, too, a man got to know exactly if a cannon-shot was making in his direction; sometimes the bombardment went on for days on both sides without any apparent result. There was the Naval Brigade—you would have liked to see them, Captain, in the Twenty-one Gun Battery under Captain Peel, the coolest officer in the whole navy—they were handier with the guns, and a great deal readier than our men.

"In front of the battery were the trenches, and in advance of the trenches were the rifle-pits. You could see before you the venomous little Russian pits out of which so many brave fellows were killed, dotted about with sandbags, and where the Russians lay watching our men working from parallel to parallel, and in the zigzags. There was one rifle-pit in particular—I shall come to it directly—which gave us more annoyance than any other, on account of its position. It was close to the Quarries. The fire from it interfered with the approach of our trenches, and we had lost our men in numbers in the advanced sap at this point. It was for the moment the *bête noir* of our engineer officers. Of course, you have read in the papers what sort of work we have had in the trenches. On a quiet night, when the batteries were silent and the weather fair, it was pleasant enough. We sat round a fire smoking, telling yarns, or even sleeping, but always with the gun in readiness. In wet and bad weather it was a different thing, however. Remember that we only had ammunition boots, made by contract, which gave out after a week. The mud got trodden about deeper and deeper, till it was pretty well up to the knees: and when snow fell on top of it, and rain on top of that, and all became a wet pool of thick brown mud, it was about as lively work as wading up and down the harbour at low tide, even if you did happen to have a "rabbit," that is, one of the coats lined with white fur. And if it was a hot night you had the pleasure of listening to the cannonade, and could see nothing on the Russian side but the continuous flash of the guns. And there was always the excitement of a possible sortie.

"We went out for night work in the trenches with heavy hearts, I can tell you, and many a man wished it were day again, and he was back in safety. We grew every day more badly off, too. Not only did the boots give out, but the greatcoats dropped to pieces, and the commissariat fell short. You have heard all that story. Jack of the Naval Brigade did not mind so much as regards the greatcoats, because he could patch and mend. He used to sell his slops for brandy, and cobble his old garments with the brown canvas of the sandbags. But the redcoats were not so handy—I have often thought it a great pity that our fellows don't imitate the sailors, and learn how to do things for themselves—we suffered terribly. That you know, too; and any national conceitedness about the pluck of our fellows in fighting so well under such conditions has to be pulled up by the thought that what we did the French and Russians did, too. After all, there is no such thing as one nation being braver than another."

"Our sailors were stronger than the French," said the Captain. "When it came to pounding with the big guns, they held out longer."

"Let me come to my piece of great good fortune," Leonard went on, "or I shall be talking all night. I have told you of the rifle-pit by the Quarries which caused us such a lot of trouble. Now I am going to tell you how I took it. It was an afternoon in April, 1855. We were in the trenches; there had been joking with a lot of 'griffs,' young recruits just out from England; the men used to show them the immense wooden spoons with which the Russian soldiers eat their coarse black bread soaked in water, and declare, to Johnny Raw's terror, that the Russians had mouths to correspond. At that time the fighting between rifle-pits was the great feature of the siege, and to take a rifle-pit was one of the most deadly things possible, as it was also the most important. The 'griffs' went down to the most advanced trench; some of them had never been under fire before, and they were naturally nervous. Just after grog time—their grog had been taken down to them—a heavy firing began, and one of those curious panics which sometimes seize some veteran soldiers attacked these boys, and they bolted; left the trench and skulked back along the zigzag, declaring that the enemy was out in force. That was nonsense, and I was ordered down with a dozen men to take their place. My fellows, I remember, chuckled at finding the grog still there, and made short work of it.

"We had not been in the trench very long before a sortie in force actually took place. We were in front of the Redan; before us, under the Redan, stood the pit of which I have told you; on the right was the Malakoff. Suddenly a cannonade *d'enfer* began from the Mamelon and the Malakoff, and we began to suspect that something was going to happen; and then, between the two forts, we saw the advance of the great Russian sortie. To our great joy, they turned to the left, in the direction of the French. While we looked, a thought came into my head—an inspiration. I reflected that the holders of the enemy's rifle-pit would very likely be watching their own sortie, and that now was the moment to make an attempt. I took half-a-dozen of our men; we crept out of cover, and then, without a word, rushed across the ground between. It was as I thought: the Russians never saw us coming: they were watching their own friends, and we were on them—a dozen of them—before they knew what had happened. It was hand-to-hand fighting, but we were the assailants. You know, Captain, it is always better to be in the attacking force. I cannot give you the details; but in less time than it takes me to tell the story, the Russians were *hors de combat* and the rifle-pit was ours. Then came the turning of the position. You understand, Celia, that the rifle-pit was a little advanced kind of redoubt, consisting of perhaps a dozen gabions filled with earth and topped with sand-bags, enough to shelter two or three dozen men. These were of course all placed in front, towards the enemy. We had to reverse the position, and place them towards the Redan. By this time we were observed, and shots began to fly about. That was the most dangerous moment of my life. We worked steadily and swiftly, tearing up the gabions, lugging the sand-bags round, getting such protection as we could while we worked. I do not know how long it lasted, but by the time we had finished there was only myself and one other left and he was wounded in the right wrist. But the rifle-pit was ours, and our men in the trench behind were cheering like madmen."

CHAPTER XII.

LEONARD CONTINUES HIS STORY.

LEONARD stopped for a moment. The Captain's eyes were kindling with the light of battle, Celia's with the light of admiration.

"It did not take long to do. It takes no time to tell. The whole thing was a happy accident; but it was the one fortunate moment of my life. Our men, watching from the trenches, cheered again; a rush was made, and that rifle-pit never went back to the Russians."

"They ought to have given you the Victoria Cross, Leonard," I cried.

"No, no," he replied, "that was given for braver actions than mine. Captain Bouchier got it for taking the 'Ovens,' a rifle-pit which could hold a couple of hundred; such gallant fellows as Private Beckle, of the 41st, who stood over the body of his wounded Colonel against a dozen of the enemy—those are the things that make a man V.C. As for me, I was more than rewarded, as you shall hear.

"When we came off trench duty, and were marched to our own quarters, I was sent for by the Colonel. You may judge what I felt when he told me, after speaking of the affair in the kindest manner, that he should take care it was properly reported. He was better than his word, because the next day he ordered me to attend in the morning at Lord Raglan's head-quarters. I went up in trembling, but I had no occasion to fear. All the Generals were there, for a Council was to be held that day. General Burgoyne, when I was called in, very kindly explained to the Chief the importance of this rifle-pit, and how its occupation by our men would facilitate matters in our advanced approaches towards the Redan, and then he told Marshal Pelissier and Omar Pasha in French, and in the handsomest terms, what I had done. Lord Raglan spoke a few words to my Colonel, and then he said, in his quiet, steady way, what I shall never forget.

"'Sergeant Coplestone, you have done a gallant action, and I hear a good report of you. I shall recommend you to the Field-Marshal Commanding-in-Chief for promotion. I am sure you will not disgrace Her Majesty's Commission.'

"I could not speak—indeed, it was not for me to speak. I saluted, and retired. Those words of the gallant old Chief—and that scene—I can never forget."

"Tell us," said Celia, "what he was like, Lord Raglan?"

"He was a grand old man," said Leonard, "with a grave face, squarely cut about the chin, over-hanging brows, deep-set eyes, and wavy white hair gone off at the temples; his nose was aquiline, and the expression of his face was one of great beauty. Every one trusted him, the French and Turks as much as the English. He had left one arm in the Peninsular War thirty years before, and he was about sixty-nine years of age. He was never so happy, his staff used to say, as when he was under fire, and yet he was careful of his soldiers' lives.

What killed him was disappointment at his failure of the 18th June. He wanted to wipe out the memory of Waterloo from the minds of French and English by a victory as brilliantly attained by both armies side by side on the anniversary of that battle. It was a muddle and a mess. What was to be the grand success of the campaign proved the most serious reverse that the allied armies experienced in the Crimea. Out of five general officers commanding columns four were killed or mortally wounded, and out of one small force fifteen hundred gallant fellows were killed on that terrible day. Death was very busy with us just then. General Estcourt, Adjutant-General, a splendid man, and worthy companion in arms with Lord Raglan, died a week later. Captain Lyons, the son of Sir Edmund, died about the same day; on Thursday, the 28th, the Chief himself expired; and Colonel Vico, the French Aide-de-Camp, attached to the English headquarters, died also after this event, showing the depressing influence of even a temporary defeat on the best of men. Even one of the interpreters sickened and sank. It was a sort of murrain among those at headquarters.

"Well," Leonard went on after a pause, "that is all newspaper news. What the papers could not tell you was the grief of both armies and the profound sensation caused by Lord Raglan's death. There may have been better generals in the history of England's wars, but there never was one more loved and trusted. His life was perfectly simple; his headquarters contained nothing but camp furniture, a table on trestles, a red table-cloth, camp-chairs, and no carpets; he was up at all hours, and he was without fear.

"Of the other generals I think Pelissier was the best. He was a little dumpy man, with a thick neck, and he was a little too fond of hurling his men at the enemy, but he did fight, and fought well. They made him Duke of Malakoff afterwards, which is as if we were to make a man Duke of Jones."

"Why?"

"Because the Malakoff was named after a man who had once kept a tavern on the spot. Malakoff was a purser in the Russian Navy, and being kicked out of the service for drinking, swindling, and smuggling,—this last he did in smuggling ship's stores. came ashore and started a drink-shop outside

Sebastopol, where he could combine profit with the pursuit of his favourite occupation. And as his drink was cheaper than could be got anywhere else, for he had the advantage of his old smuggling experiences in the laying in of his stores, the place became a favourite resort of the Russian sailors when they came ashore to get drunk. After a while the stony hill with Malakoff's sheebeen upon it, became Malakoff's Redoubt. Sturdy Pelissier, however, did not look much like a duke, as we picture dukes. When Soyer the cook came out, he was so like the General that we used to ask which was the cook and which was the General. Only Soyer wore more gold lace, and distinguished himself in that way.

"My commission came out before the death of Lord Raglan. You may fancy what a trial it was to me, on that day, not to be able to write home, and tell you all about it. I did write, however; I wrote a full history of all I had done, with a note inside that it was to be sent to you, Captain, in case I fell. My brother officers gave me a hearty welcome, and we had a big dinner—as big as the materials at our disposal allowed, the day I joined

—so to speak. I have been to many a better feast since, but none at which I was so entirely happy. I remember that the things to eat were scanty, as often happened in the year 1855—but I was eating what there was among gentlemen, with Her Majesty's commission in my pocket. We had no candlesticks fit to show on a mess table, but a dozen bayonets, with candles in them, stuck in the table, made a brilliant illumination."

Leonard paused again.

"The dinner was the last that some of us were to take together. On the 18th of June came our Repulse at the Redan, when we lost half-a-dozen from our mess.

"As soon as quiet days came I took an opportunity of telling the Colonel my little history—how I was ignorant of my parentage, how I was a gutter child, wandering about the streets, living on the charity of a kind and good woman, herself poor, and how the Captain picked me up, educated me—and allowed me to go out into the world to seek my fortune; how I was to get home after five years, if I could, to report myself, and how my dream had been to go home, somehow, as a gentleman."

"Always the best of old Captains," said Celia, patting the old man's cheek.

"Nonsense, my dear," said the Captain. "Best of boys, you mean. Go on, Leonard."

"The Colonel will call on you to-morrow, sir. You will remember that he has been my constant and most steady friend and adviser throughout."

"Ay—ay," said the Captain. "I shall find something to say to him. Go on."

"Of all the fifty fellows that made up our mess when I got the colours, there are not a dozen left now. The winters, the trench-work, the night-work, and its after effects, killed those whom the Russian bullets spared. They fell around me, and I passed through it unharmed; we were in almost everything, and I think every man in the regiment did his duty, sir, as well as any of your old sea captains."

"I doubt it not," said the Captain; "we belong to a fighting people."

"And so we finished that war and came home again. I was a Lieutenant, when we landed at this very port and marched up the street, colours flying, amid the cheers of the people. I looked out for you again, sir, and for you, Celia and Laddy, but could not see any of you in the crowd. It was very hard not to call and tell you of my fortune, harder still not to ask for news of you, but only three years of the five were passed, and I had my promise to keep. We went to Chobham, and from there, after six months' rest, were ordered out to India.

"We will talk about the Mutiny another time. I got my company, as I had got my step, six months later, by death vacancies. The same good fortune followed me in India as in the Crimea. The sun did not strike me as it struck some of ours. I caught no fever or cholera which killed some, and I got through the fighting without a scratch; and the only thing that troubled me towards the end was the fear that I might not get home in time. We had a long and tedious passage, but we arrived at last, and I have kept my promise and my appointment, Celia."

After the first surprise the Captain took the stories of the fighting with unconcern. In the matter of battles he was a fatalist, like all men who have been in action. Every bullet has its billet; there is a time for every man; skulkers always get the worst of it—these were the simple axioms of his nautical creed. That Leonard should have gained a commission was to him so surprising an event as to swallow up all minor things. That he should have borne himself bravely was only what he expected, and that he should have been spared to return was the special act of Providence in return for many prayers for which he had given thanks already.

But to Celia—

> "'Twas passing strange;
> 'Twas pitiful, 'twas wondrous pitiful."

Leonard was no longer her old friend, her playmate, the boy to whom she had looked as a girl for protection, help, and guidance; he was now a man who had looked in the face of Death and quailed not. For the first time she talked with one who had fought in the way which had, so to speak, surrounded her later years.

She took the medals again, when Leonard completed his tale, and kissed them reverently with glittering eyes before she gave them back to him.

"Leonard," she said, "when Laddy and I used

to wonder where you were, and what you were doing, we never thought of this."

"And when we worked ourselves up into rages about the poor army starving in the cold of the Crimea, Cis," I said, "we never thought that Leonard was among them."

"We were all blind bats," said the Captain, "not to guess where he would go and what he would become. The only true profession for a gentleman is the profession of arms. There's no opening for volunteers in the navy, as there used to be, more's the pity. Cloudesley Shovel got on in that way, and in the good old times, Leonard, you might have risen to be a First Lieutenant by this."

"Are you not satisfied, sir?" asked Leonard, with a smile.

"Satisfied, my boy! Celia, my dear, tell him for me what we think."

Celia blushed very prettily.

"We are so proud and happy, Leonard," she said, "that we hardly know what we are saying. In all our talks about you we never hoped that you would be able to tell such a tale as this."

"Never," I repeated.

"We knew, did we not, Captain, that Leonard would bear himself bravely?"

"Ay, ay," said the Captain, laying his hand on Leonard's shoulder, "that we knew all along. We know sneaks and skulkers when we see them. Malingerers carry the truth in their faces, and by the same rule we know whom we can trust. Leonard and Laddy belong to them."

It was very good of the old fellow to say a word for me. Not that I wanted it, but it showed that he was anxious that I should not feel left out in the cold.

"Go on, Celia, my pretty," said the Captain; "is there any more to say?"

"No, sir," Celia replied. "Only—only——" And here her voice broke down, and her eyes filled with tears. "Only to thank God, Leonard, again and again, and all our lives, for keeping you safe through all these dangers, and for bringing you back to the Captain and to Laddy—and to Mrs. Jeram—and to me."

"Amen," said the Captain; "that's very well put, Celia, my dear; and if you were to stay here altogether—and I wish you would—I should promote you to be chaplain. And now, Mrs. Jeram, you and I had better go off to bed, and leave these young people to talk as long as they will. It's past twelve o'clock, ma'am. Kiss me, pretty. Laddy, we've got something to talk about now, you and I, in winter evenings. Leonard, my son, good-night." He rested his hand on Leonard's head. "I am so glad, my lad; I am so glad."

They went away, and we three were left alone.

It was a night of full moon, without a cloud in the sky. We took our chairs into the garden and sat under the old mulberry tree, facing the mill-dam lake, and talked.

We talked all the brief night, while the bright moon hid the stars, and we could only faintly distinguish Charles's Wain slowly moving round the Polar light, until the moon herself was paled by the grey of the early morning, and even long after the sun had lifted his head above the sky, and was pouring upon the sheet of water, making the little island redoubt upon it stand out clear cut against the sky, with a foreground of deep black shade.

What had we to talk about? Our hearts burned within us, even like those of the disciples at Emmaus. We three who had grown up together and loved each other,—we were met again, and all in early man and womanhood, and we loved each other still. I, with my jealous eye, watched Celia, and could see the sweet shy look that told me, what indeed I knew before, how only a word was wanted to flash a spark into a flame, how but a touch was needed before a maiden would yield. I saw, too, Leonard's eyes stealing every moment to rest upon her sweet face. It was with a natural pang that I saw this. Nobody knew, better than I, that Celia could be nothing to me but my dear sister, my true and most trusted friend. I had battled with my passion, and it was dead. Now, I was ashamed of it. Who but Leonard was worthy of that sweet girl? She had no fault, nor has she any still, in my eyes. She is altogether incomparable. And who but Leonard, our hero, our Perseus, was fit to claim her for his own, love her, marry her, and keep her safe in his arms? Did I, sometimes, have thoughts, angry thoughts, of what might have been? Perhaps, we are but human; but on the whole I had learned by that time to look on Celia as my sister.

From time to time Leonard asked us about ourselves. We fenced with his question. It was not the season to parade Celia's troubles, nor mine. We were there to listen to his story, to be gladdened by his successes. What good to be talking of ourselves when every moment seemed sacred to his welcome home? The broad daylight found us still talking. Celia's eyes were brighter, her cheek a little paler. Leonard was handsomer, I think, by day than he had seemed by the light of our modest pair of candles. I went to the larder, and found there a whole chicken, with the Captain's second bottle of champagne, and we had a late supper, or an early breakfast, at four, with no one to look at us but the sparrows, who peeped over the housetops and chirped to each other that there would be a most unusual and festive chance in the way of crumbs as soon as the foolish humans should go to bed.

We should have sat till breakfast-time, but that Leonard looked at his watch and sprang to his feet.

"Cis," he cried, quite in his old tones, "do you know what time it is? Half-past five. You must go to bed, if only for a couple of hours. Good-night—till nine o'clock." He held her hand in his. "And—and—look in your glass when you go to your room—and think if I could have expected our little Cis to grow into—what you see there."

She shook her head, but did not answer, only holding out her hand timidly. But she was not displeased.

Then she ran away and left us.

"Laddy, old boy," said Leonard, "one doesn't come home to be made much of every day. I can't sleep if I go to bed. What are we to do?"

"Let us go out to the Castle and bathe, and be back by eight when the Captain gets up."

"We will, Laddy. How splendid the dear old Captain is looking! Is there anybody like him in the world? And Celia——" Here he stopped. "You remember what I told you, Laddy, when I went away? Well, I have never forgotten it, and I mean it more than ever."

CHAPTER XIII.

A FRIENDLY CHAT.

"HOW fresh it is! And how jolly to be back in the old place!" Leonard cried, as we walked out into the silent streets.

Half-past five. The best part of the summer day. There was no one stirring yet, save here and there an early housemaid brushing away the morning dew upon the doorstep. Our feet echoed on the pavement with a clatter from wall to wall as if of many hundred feet, and when we spoke it was as if our voices were too loud as they reverberated along the houses. All just as it had been of old so many times when we two boys had run along the streets at six for a swim in the sea before school. Nothing changed save that the boy who used to run and jump, shouting in the overflow of strength and spirits, rejoicing in the breath of life, was become the splendid fellow who strode at my side. Of course I was just the same. A sleeping city and two boys going out to bathe. Nothing changed. The town asleep, and my brain filled with all sorts of weird fancies. I have read of deserted and ruined cities in the far-east Syrian plains, on the edge of the great and terrible wilderness where the lion of prophecy roams round the heaps of Kouyounjik. Some of these cities still stand, with their rooms and their staircases perfect as when the terrified inhabitants fled before some conquering Shalmaneser who came from the mysterious east destroying as he went. Now there is not a single soul left to mourn over the greatness of the past. You may hear the cry of the lizard, the shrill voice of the cigale; your feet echo as you stride along the silent footway, and you speak in a whisper, for this is an image of Death the conqueror. As I go along with Leonard I somehow think of these old ruins. There is no connection between a ruined Syrian city and a sleeping modern town, except the stillness which smites the soul as you pass along deserted pavements between houses closed and barred, which might be houses bereft of their inhabitants, soulless, empty, haunted. Within, the children lying asleep ; the little faces flushed with sleep, and the little limbs tossed carelessly upon the sheets, the wondering eyes just about to waken for the glories and fresh joys of another day. Within, the young men and the maidens, the old men and the ancient dames, each wrapped in the solemn loneliness of sleep, when spirits even of lovers dwell apart, while the busy fingers of the restless Fates are weaving the many-coloured web and weft of life's short story. What stories behind those shutters! What dreams in those white-blinded rooms! What babble of infant voices to welcome the new-born day!

"What are you thinking of, Laddy? Dreamer, your eyes are always far away. This is just what we used to do years ago. Up at six and out across the common for a bathe! And you always dreaming! Look! there is the early bird. Good-morning, Molly. Fine morning for doorsteps—good for the complexion."

"Get along o' your nonsense," said Molly, not displeased.

"She's quite right; you are an officer now, Leonard, and it can't be allowed any more."

"Where is your mop, Molly?" he went on, with his light, boyish laugh.

"Mops have gone out," I replied, "so have pattens."

"Have they, really? Not the dear old mop that they used to trundle up and down their arms? I'm sorry for it, Laddy. The domestic mop used to be as good a weapon for the defence of housemaidenhood as any. And in a seaport town, too. Many is the time I have seen a too demonstrative Jack discomfited by a timely dab in the face from a dripping mop. Slaps and scratches are poor things compared with a dollop of wet mop. Even a Billingsgate broadside cannot be so effective. Something might be done, I dare say, with a garden hose, but, after all, nothing like a mop and a bucket. And even pattens gone, too,—the tinkling patten. I wonder no love-sick poet ever celebrated the musical clatter on the stones of the housemaid's patten. These are the losses of civilisation, Laddy."

We passed through the gate, our heels clanking across the iron drawbridge. Beyond the bridge, and between the walls and the advanced works, was the guard-house, where stood a sentry, who saluted us with as much astonishment as discipline would allow, expressed upon a not remarkably mobile set of features. Why should an officer, who was not obliged to stand at a sentry-box during the small hours, be up and out so early? What good, in such a case, of being an officer at all?

And then we passed the awkward squad on their way to goose-step drill. They saluted, too, as we passed. The salute of those days was a thing of ceremony—extension of right arm, doubling of right elbow, hand square to the forehead, return double, drop of right arm. The Marines did it best, regulating the motions from a slovenly and irregular movement of the arm for a middy or a mate to a precise and clearly directed six-fold ceremonial, ending with a resonant slap of the right leg, for superior rank. They knew, the Marines, how to signify respect to rank. Any popular officer, particularly if he was also an Admiral, was saluted as he went down the street with a regular Kentish fire of open-handed slaps of right legs. That also is a thing of the past.

"I was like those honest fellows once," said our young Captain gravely. "One of the awkward squad; sentry in the barracks; one of the rank and file; standing up to be drilled and ordered. Well; it's not a bad thing for a man."

"And the officers of the regiment, Leonard;—did that make any difference?"

"I became at once one of themselves—a brother officer. What else could their treatment be? I asked the Colonel, as a personal favour, to tell them who I was. Every regiment has its 'rankers;' every ranker has his story. I should be a snob if I were ashamed of having risen."

We crossed the broad common, where all the old furze had by this time been cut down and cleared away to make room for military evolutions; and we came to the castle standing upon the edge of the sea. There was not a soul upon the beach, not even our old friend the cursing coastguard; we sat down under the slope of stone, for it was now low tide, and made ready for a dip.

"There go the last fumes of last night's long talk. Sitting up all night, even with Celia, *does* fog the brain a bit." Thus Leonard, coming out of the water all glorious like Apollo. I suppose it is because I am so unshapely that I think so much of beauty of form. Then we dressed, and Leonard took out a cigar-case, to my astonishment, for somehow I had never thought of him in connection with tobacco—heroes of imagination neither smoke nor drink wine, as we all know—and then lying back on the shingle, he began to talk lazily.

"I am rather tired of telling about myself, Laddy; it is your turn now."

Of course I knew it was coming, sooner or later.

"You do not expect to hear much about me," I said. "I am organist at St. Faith's; that is my official position, and it brings me in six-and-twenty pounds a year. For ten shillings a week I hear three services on Sunday and two in the week."

"Poor old boy!" said Leonard. "Can't something better be got?"

"I rather like the church work. Then I give lessons in music and singing, and out of them I make about two hundred a year more."

"I see. But the house does not seem much improved by this enormous accession of wealth."

"No. The fact is, Leonard, that the Captain

takes all the money, and I never ask what he does with it. If I made a thousand a year I am certain that extravagant old man would absorb it all."

"Ah! The crafty old Captain! Do you think he invests it in Russian stock or Turkish bonds?"

"No. I think he gives it away. Where does he go when every morning he disappears for three hours? Answer me that, Captain Leonard."

"He always did it, and he always will. He is an incorrigible old mystery."

"In the afternoon he stays at home, unless it is half-holiday, when he goes out on the common to see the boys play, and talk to them with his hands behind his back. To be sure he knows every boy in the town."

Leonard laughed.

"I remember an incident or two—years ago—when we were children in the house. There was a woman—she had black hair, I know—and she used to come in the evening and ask for money. I suppose, from my personal experience, that she was drunk one night when she came, and went on—I forget what about—like another Jezebel. She wanted money, and the Captain was so upset by her inconsiderate conduct that he—behaved as the Captain always does."

"What was that?"

"Went to the Sailing Directions. Remembered that every sinner had to be forgiven at least seventy times seven, and so added one more to her score, which I should say must have already reached a pretty high total. He gives his money all away, Laddy, and if I were you I would not work too hard, because he will only give yours away too. The kind old man! What else have you to tell us about yourself?"

"I've been taking care of Cis," I said, evading the difficulty.

"So I saw last night. Good care, Laddy. There never was a better brother than you."

But he did not know all; and I could not tell him how near I had been, once, to betraying his trust.

"Cis—Celia—Oh! Laddy!" He threw away the cigar and started to his feet, gazing out to sea. "Did Heaven ever make a sweeter girl? Did you watch her face last night? And her eyes, how they softened and brightened!"

"Am I blind, Leonard?"

"Did you see how she lit up with pity and sympathy? Laddy, I must win that girl, or I shall not care what happens.

"I have never ceased thinking of her," he went on; "never since I left you five years ago. To be sure, when I was a private soldier, or even a non-commissioned officer, it seemed too absurd to think of her, but when my promotion came, then the old thoughts revived. All through the war I thought of her. In those dreadful nights when we sat and slept in the trenches, knee-deep in trampled mud and melting snow, I used to let my thoughts wander back to this old place. Always in Celia's Arbour, lying beneath the elms: play-acting beside the gun: running up and down the slopes with little Cis, wondering what she was like. You with her too, of course, with your great dreamy eyes and trusty face—Laddy and Cis. I suppose it was sentimental, all of it; but I am different from most men. There is no family life for you and me to look back on except that. In those days—I am not boasting—I had no fear, because it seemed as if every day brought me nearer to her, and higher up the ladder. In case of death I had a letter written to the Captain, enclosing one for you and one for Celia, telling you all about it. But I did not die. Then I had to come home and be near you, within a hundred miles, and yet not go to see you; that was very hard. When India came I lost my old fearlessness, and began to be anxious. It was want of faith, I suppose. At all events I escaped, and came out of the whole racket unwounded. Laddy, I should be worse than an infidel," he added, solemnly, "if I did not see in my five years of fortune the protection of the Lord."

"We pray—we who stay at home—for the safety of those who go abroad; and perhaps our prayers are sometimes granted. Is that sentiment, too?" I asked.

He was silent for a little space; then he shook himself as one who would change the current of his thoughts.

"Let us get back, old boy; the Captain will be up by this time. And now tell me more about yourself; there must be more to tell than that you have become a musician. Haven't you fallen in love, Laddy?"

"Fallen in love! Who is there to fall in love with a man like me? Look at my shadow, Leonard."

It was a gruesome-looking shadow, with high back, and head thrust forward. I think that if Peter Schlemihl had been hump-backed he would have made an easier bargain for the rolling up and putting away of his shadow. A small annuity, paid quarterly, would have been considered ample on the part of the purchaser. And as for awkward questions—well—there are secrets in every family, and it would soon be understood that the absence of shadow must not be remarked upon. I only know that my own was a constant shame and humiliation to me. Unless I walked with my face to the sun there was no getting out of the deformity.

"Bah! You and your shadow. Laddy, look in the glass. You have eyes that would steal away the heart of Penelope, and a musical voice, and you are a genius."

"Nonsense. I am only a plain musician, and as for falling in love, have I not been every day with Celia? How could I fall in love with any other girl when I had known her?"

"That is true," he said reflectively. "That is quite true. Who could? She is altogether sweet and lovely. After dreaming of her every day for five years I am afraid of her. And you have been with her, actually with her, for five years."

I think he guessed my secret, for he laid his hand affectionately on my shoulder.

"Cis and I are brother and sister," I said; "that you know very well. But you are right to be afraid of her. Men ought to be afraid of such a girl. Only the priest, you know," I added, following up a little train of allegory that arose in my mind, "can touch the Ark of the Lord."

"You mean——"

"I mean that a man ought to be holy before he ventures upon holy ground."

"Yes; you are a Puritan, Laddy, but you are quite right. I have been saying to myself ever since she left us, 'She is only a woman after all.' And yet that does not seem to bring her any closer to me. It would bring all other women closer, but not Celia."

"She is only a woman to two men, Leonard, and to those two a woman of flesh and blood, with all sorts of hopes and fancies. One of these is myself, her brother, and the other—will be the man she loves. But there is a great trouble, and you ought to learn what it is."

I told him, in as few words as I could manage, part of the story. It seemed a breach of trust to tell him what I *knew*—though Celia only feared it—that this German had a hold upon Mr. Tyrrell which he threatened to use; but I was obliged to let him understand that Mr. Tyrrell wished her to accept the man, and I told how Celia suffered from the assiduity with which he followed her about, went to church with her, was everywhere seen with her, and how he hoped gradually to overcome, by quiet perseverance, the dislike which she, as well as her friends, would at first show to the marriage.

"He has not yet pressed for a reply," I concluded. "But he will very soon now."

"Why now?"

I omit the remarks (which were un-Christian) made by Leonard during my narrative.

"Because you have come home. Because he will find out that Celia sat up all night with us talking. Because he will see her looking happier and brighter, and will suspect the cause."

"The cause, Laddy? Do you mean——"

"I mean nothing but that Celia is glad to see you back again, and if you expected anything less you must be very forgetful of little Cis Tyrrell. If you expected anything more, Leonard—why—perhaps you had better speak to her yourself."

"I remember Herr Räumer," Leonard went on. "He was always hanging about the streets with his blue spectacles and his big white moustache. I remember him almost as early as I remember anything. They used to say he was an exile from Germany for Republican opinions. During that year I spent learning French and Russian in the Polish Barrack he took an opportunity of speaking to me, was very friendly once or twice, and took a great interest in the Poles. I remember he wanted to know what they talked about. I wonder if he is a Russian spy?"

"Nonsense, Leonard. He dislikes the Russians."

"Does he? My dear Laddy, you know nothing about the country whose people are so pleasant, and whose government is so detestable. Russian spies are everywhere. The Russian Secret Service is like a great net spread over the whole world; they are the Jesuits of politics. Herr Räumer may not be one of the black gang, but he may be; and if he isn't, I should like to find out what keeps a German in this place, where we have got a great dockyard, and where improvements and new inventions are always being tried and talked of, where there are several regiments, half our fleet, and a lot of Poles. Do you think it is love of the town?"

"I suppose he is used to it," I said.

"What kind of man is he?"

"He is a cynic. He professes to live for his own enjoyment, and nothing else. Says the rest is humbug. I have never heard him say a generous thing, or acknowledge a generous motive. Yet he talks well, and one likes to be with him."

"I shall call upon him," said Leonard. "As for his own enjoyment and the selfish theory of philosophy, a good many Germans affect that kind of thing. They think it philosophical and intellectual, and above their fellow-creatures, to be wrapped in a cloak of pure selfishness. Well, Laddy, unless Celia wishes it——"

"She does not wish it."

"She shall not throw herself away upon this man. Great Heavens! my beautiful Celia," he said, "my beautiful Celia, to be thrown to an old ——" He checked himself. "No use getting angry. But if there is no other way of stopping it, we'll carry her off, Laddy, you and I together, and stand the racket afterwards. I can't very well call him out and shoot him. I don't mean that I see at present how it is to be prevented, but we will find out."

"Perseus," I said, "had to borrow of other people two or three little things to help him when he went on that expedition of his. You had better take the Captain, as well as myself, into your confidence. Here we are at home, and there is the jolly old Captain at the door, beaming on us like the morning sun."

"Come in, boys," he shouted, "come in to breakfast. Celia is ready, and so am I. Ho! ho! I am so glad, Leonard. I am so glad."

CHAPTER XIV.

A TRIUMPHAL PROCESSION.

THESE were the days of a grand triumphal procession, in which we led our hero about to be congratulated by his friends. There were not many of these, it is true. That made it all the better, because the chances of the hateful passion of envy being aroused were lessened. To be sure, there were none who could be envious. Leonard's road to honour is a Royal road, open to all. But it is beset with difficulties. Stout is the heart and strong the will of him who dares to tread that pipe-clayed and uncertain way. None of the boys with whom we had been at school knew Leonard as a friend, or even as an old acquaintance. The reserved school boy who fought his way to freedom from molestation was not likely now to search out the lads who had once stung his proud soul by references to the price of soap. They were now chiefly engaged in promoting the commercial interests of the town, and would have saluted the young officer had they known who he was, hat in hand.

We went round, therefore, among our little circle of friends.

Mr. Broughton promptly invited us to dinner.

There were present at the banquet—to furnish it forth all the resources of the reverend gentleman's cellar were put under contribution—the Captain, Mr. Pontifex, Leonard, and myself. The dinner was simple, consisting of salmon, lamb, and chicken, cutlets, with early peas and asparagus. A little light Sauterne, which his reverence recommended in preference to sherry, as leaving the palate clean for the port, accompanied the meal. There was also champagne, which, he said, was a wine as Catholic as the Athanasian Creed, inasmuch as it goes equally well with a simple luncheon of cold chicken, and with the most elaborate Gaudy. After dinner, solely in deference to the uncorrupted digestion of youth, he ordered a dish of strawberries.

"It is not the right time to eat them," he said, in a voice almost as solemn for the occasion as that of Mr. Pontifex. "Their proper place is after breakfast. A good dinner biscuit would be better. But young men expect these things. When you and I were undergraduates, Pontifex, we liked them." And then, while we absorbed the strawberries, he arose and brought from a sideboard, with great care and with his own hands, four decanters of port.

They stood all in a row before him, a label hanging from each. He put out his hands over them like a priest pronouncing a blessing.

"We ought, brother Pontifex," he said, "to have a form of thanksgiving for port."

"When I was a young man," said Mr. Pontifex, with a sigh, "I was called by some of my reckless companions—ahem!—Two-Bottle Pontifex. . . . . Two-Bottle Pontifex—such was my appetite for port-wine at that period! I am now never allowed by Mrs. Pontifex—alas!—even to taste the—ahem! —the beverage."

"This," said Mr. Broughton, affectionately caressing one of the decanters, "is a bottle of 1820. I sincerely wish, Leonard, that I could entertain the hope of bequeathing you a few dozens in token of regard to my old pupil. But I have not more than enough for my own use, always supposing that I reach the allotted time of three score years and ten. It is generous still, this wine." He poured out a glass, and held it to the light. "Mark the colour; refresh yourself with this bouquet; taste the noble wine. He suited the action to the recommendation. "What a combination of delight for all the senses at once! Nature never raised a sweeter colour—a more divine fragrance—a more Olympian taste than she has united——"

"Under Providence, brother Broughton," said Mr. Pontifex, shaking his head.

"—united in this one glass of the finest wine ever grown. How my good grandfather, the Bishop—whose piety was only equalled by his taste for port—would have enjoyed this moment! The day before he died, his chaplain, on pouring him out his single glass—the Bishop was then too feeble for more—said, 'We shall drink, my lord, in a better world, a more delicious wine.' He was a learned and sound divine, but young, and with a palate comparatively untrained. 'We cannot,' said the good old Bishop. 'Better wine than this is not to be had.'"

"The next decanter," he went on with a sigh for the good Bishop's memory, "is a bottle of 1834. I do not know aright how to sing its praises. After what I have said of 1820 I would only say—

"'O matre pulchra, filia pulchrior!'

You shall taste it presently. Thirteen years later, we come to 1847. What a year for port! and to think that it should be followed—that year of generous and glorious vintages—by the year of rebellion and social upheaving! As if Heaven's choicest blessings were altogether thrown away upon ungrateful man! The last is a bottle of 1851, now four years in bottle and still a little too full. The four bottles do not make altogether a bottle a head—nothing to your old days, Pontifex—but we three are advanced in years, I am sorry to think, and the boys have been trained in a different school. Perhaps a better one.

"And now," he resumed, looking round with smiles twinkling in his eyes and playing over his jolly red face, "a Toast. The health of Leonard

—our brave lad who has come home from the wars with medals and honours which make us all proud of him. It was in this room, my dear boy, that you first read the wars of antiquity told in heroic verse. It was here that your ear and your heart became attuned to the glorious aspects of heroism, and the din of battle. Remember, when you have some of your own, that nothing succeeds like putting a boy through the good old mill of Homer and Virgil. You were educated by me for your work, not by cramming yourself with a bundle of scientific facts, which they would persuade us is what soldiers want, but by the deeds of the great men of Greece and Rome. You have not forgotten Diomede, I hope."

"No, sir," said Leonard. "Nor Sarpedon, nor the cowardly Paris, nor Turnus, nor Nisus and Euryalus—nor any of them. Who can forget the jolly old battles?"

"When I was a schoolboy," Mr. Pontifex said, solemnly, "I once fought a battle with another boy in which, I remember, I was worsted, owing to the superior strength of my antagonist. This breach of rules was subsequently discovered by the master of the school, and I was summoned before his presence. As I had nothing to say in—ahem!—vindication of the offence, I was instantly condemned to be—ahem!—in fact—birched! The—the necessary preliminaries having been performed, they proceeded to search for the rod, an instrument which was kept for that purpose under wet straw in the garden. When this had been found, I sustained a most fearful infliction."

We all laughed at this graphic reminiscence of a school battle and its consequences, and Mr. Broughton bade us charge our glasses and begin the '34. Mr. Pontifex grew more solemn as well as paler under the influence of the port as the evening went on, and Mr. Broughton more purple in the face, more jolly, and more animated. I had frequently seen this opposite effect of wine upon both clergymen. After the second bottle, the wine passed chiefly from one to the other, because the Captain had already exceeded a double ration and Leonard was moderate in his libations.

In the course of the evening, the Perpetual Curate of St. Faith's pronounced a eulogium on the world generally, on those who know how to enjoy life, and on the good things life has to give. It was in the middle of the last bottle, and his face was a deep purple, while Mr. Pontifex, perfectly white, sat with his long upper lip grown half an inch longer, and the solemnity of Rhadamanthus upon his brow.

"What good things they are," he said, enthusiastically, "to those few who know how to cultivate their senses. Wine such as this; the meats and fruits which come in their season; music such as Laddy here can play; the poetry of those divine men who made the language of a little peninsula survive for ever to fill our hearts with wonder and delight; the beauty of women to take us out of ourselves when we are young—you have been in love, Captain?"

The Captain laughed.

"Was there ever a sailor," he asked, "who has not been in love? And was there ever a lover like a sailor? What does the song say?" The Captain lifted up his pipe.

"'And the toast—for 'twas Saturday night—
Some sweetheart or wife whom he loved as his life,
Each drank and he wished he could hail her.
But the standing toast
That pleased the most

Was the wind that blows,
And the ship that goes,
And the lass that loves a sailor.' "

"And the lass that loves a sailor," echoed Mr. Broughton, to his colleague's astonishment. "I knew you had, Captain. Catch a salt neglecting such a chance of completing his education. It did you good—own that; and it did me good, too, after the fit was over. Come, Pontifex, your wife is not here. Confess."

Mr. Pontifex shook his head very solemnly, and made answer with many parentheses.

"It is a sad—sad reminiscence of an ardent and perhaps (in this and in one or two other particulars which I have already at various times, as you may remember, Johnnie, in the course of conversation touched upon) ill-regulated youth, that I once imagined myself—actually in Love"—he spoke in a tone of the greatest surprise—"with a—a—in fact—a young person of the opposite sex, who vended perfumes, unless my memory geatly deceives me, at an establishment in the High——"

"And I dare say it was a very good thing for you," returned his jovial brother, interrupting the further particulars of this amour. "It was for me, and no worse for the girl I loved, because she preferred somebody else, and married him. It was an education for us all. As it is now, Captain, at our time of life we may say—

> "'Old as we are, for ladies' love unfit,
> The power of beauty we remember yet.'

And the sight of a pretty face, like that of Celia Tyrrell—bless her!—I drink this glass of the Forty-seven to her—is like the shadow of a rock in the wilderness. Age has its pleasures; they are, besides the drinking of good port, the contemplation of beautiful women and active youth. We have lived—let us sit down and watch those who are living. You, Leonard boy," he resumed the familiar tone of our old tutor, "you had the impudence to tell me five years ago, that you would rather help to make history than to write it. And that is what you have been doing ever since. And it does us good —us old stagers, to see you doing it."

Presently he became more serious, and spoke from the Christian's point of view.

A Christian scholar and a gentleman. His race is nearly extinct now. But he had his uses, and many were his virtues. When I read Robert Browning's poem of "Bishop Blougram's Apology," I read for Blougram, Broughton. And yet he only touched that Right Reverend Father in a few points. Above all, a scholar; and with it, a kindly heart, a simple faith, and a robust, full nature which enabled him to enjoy all that could be got from life. He is gone now, with his purple face, his short fat figure, and his dogmatic sermons. I do not like the present man—who is Earnest—so well. Nor do I love the fussiness of the new school.

The next day we called upon Mrs. Pontifex, who received Leonard as cordially as that lady could make a greeting. Nothing was said about her husband's excesses in port the previous evening. She said that news had reached them of Leonard's happy return; that she rejoiced at his success, which was doubtless, she was good enough to say, deserved, though she wished it had been in more Christian fields; that the army was a bad school for those who wished to be serious; and that he must specially beware of that inflation which prosperity brings upon the heart. Then she said hospitably that she proposed, after consideration, to name an early day, for tea. Leonard laughed and accepted, leaving the day open. He always laughed, this favourite of Fortune. I do not think that festive gathering ever came off, owing to other circumstances which interfered. The Rev. John Pontifex, who was present, looking pale, and still preserving last night's solemnity, followed up the theme opened by his wife, giving us by way of illustration a few personal experiences, with copious parentheses.

"I observed the same dangerous tendency," he said, "when I was standing for my degree at Oxford; on which occasion, I may be permitted to add, though I now hope, having been chastened"—he looked at his wife—"without pride, I greatly distinguished myself"—he got a fourth. "I was treated, it is true, by the examiners with gross injustice, being required to translate passages ACTUALLY, though you may not perhaps credit the disgraceful circumstance, from the *very end* of the works both of Lucretius and Virgil!!! I was confronted, in fact, with the hardest portions of those authors." Mr. Pontifex spoke with great bitterness, and in the firm belief that Virgil, writing expressely for Academical candidates, contrived his books so as to form a series of graduated exercises. "And in spite of this I obtained a place of honourable distinction. On that occasion, I confess with repentance, my heart was greatly puff-éd up. It is an Event to look back upon with profound Repentance. I observed a similar temptation to pride, when I dealt my Blow at the Papacy in fifty-three theses. A copy of this work shall be sent to you, Leonard, before you go again into Popish regions. I heard, indeed, that one so-called Father (I suppose because he has no sons)—a Papistical Priest—had presumed to answer. He said he was an inquirer. So, indeed, am I—but—but—he is a scoundrel, and will most certainly, some day—at least, I fear so—meet with his deserts."

This seemed carrying the *odium theologicum*, as well as literary controversy, a little too far. Mr. Pontifex had but one weapon, the threat of his one punishment.

In the afternoon of what Celia called "the day after," leaving the rest of the phrase to be filled up, Leonard's Colonel called upon us. There was one thing remarkable about the Captain. He was the simplest of sailors—no retired Bo's'n could be simpler—in his habits of thought, his speech, and his way of life. But with an officer of his own or the sister service, his manner changed instinctively. To the quiet simplicity of his habitual air he added the bearing and dignity of his rank. He was, he remembered on these occasions, a Captain in the Royal Navy, and the carpet of his dining-room became a Quarter-deck.

The Colonel came to say great things of Leonard, and said them, Leonard not being present.

"He was observed by his officers, sir, from the first. Reported on his joining at his Depôt as a smart well-set-up lad. Found to be of superior rank and education to the men. Proved himself excellent at drill. Made a corporal first and a sergeant shortly after. And, sir, if it were not for his own interests, I should say I wish he was a sergeant still.

"You have heard of his gallant action, I suppose," he went on. "Nothing finer ever done. Lord Raglan sent for him, sir. He has told you that, I dare say. But he did not tell you what the chief said afterwards. It was that if he had it in his power he would have knighted him on the field of battle. He has been a credit to the regiment since the first day he joined it. We are proud of him, sir: we are proud of him, and I am happy in being able, this day, to beat up your quarters and tell you so."

The Captain answered simply. He said that Leonard was always a brave and trustworthy lad: that for his own part he had endeavoured to make the boy think of duty before all things: that it gave him unspeakable pleasure to hear what the Colonel had said and to know that it was the truth without exaggeration: that the boy was still young, and, as yet, only at the beginning of his career. I felt proud of the Captain as he made his little speech, full of dignity and good feeling.

"At all events, he owes everything to you," said the Colonel. "And now, will you dine with us to-morrow, you and Mr. Pulaski? It is guest-night."

The Captain accepted for both of us.

"I should like to ask," said the Colonel, "if it is not an impertinent question—do you think there is any chance of Copleston finding out something of his family?"

"I have thought of it more than once," the Captain replied. "His mother died in giving him birth; with the last breath she said his name was to be Leonard Copleston, 'her husband's name.' It is not a very common name. To find him one would have to consult army and navy lists of five-and-twenty years ago. If we found him, what might we not find too? That his father was a scoundrel is certain to me, from the circumstance of the boy's birth. He may be dead; he may have dishonoured the name; he may be unwilling to recognise his son—why not let things go on as they have done, without further trouble? The boy bears the Queen's Commission; he is no disgrace, but a credit to his regiment. Let us remain satisfied."

The Colonel shook his head.

"I shall look up the lists," he said. "And if I find out anything I will tell you first. If it is anything calculated to do Copleston harm, we will keep it to ourselves."

Guest-night at the Hundred-and-Twentieth. The tables covered with the regimental plate, and crowded with officers. The Colonel has our old Captain on the right, his own guest. I sit beside Leonard. The band is playing. There is a full assemblage. The younger officers are full of life and spirits. What is it like—this world I have never seen till to-night—this world of animal spirits, laughter, and careless fun? I look about me dreamily. This, then, I think, was the kind of life led by my father, Roman Pulaski, of the Imperial Guard, before Nicholas exchanged it for the Siberian mines. It must be pleasant for awhile. These young fellows are neither creating, like artists; nor criticising, like scholars; nor working for money, like professional men; nor selling their wit and spirits, like authors; nor contriving schemes for making money, like merchants; they are simply living to enjoy things. They have had a hard time of it in India: a few of them—very few, alas!—had a hard time in the Crimea: now they are back to garrison and English life, and they are rejoicing as heartily as they fought.

They tell me that the officer of to-day is scientific, and plays Kriegspiel. I am sure he is not braver, more genial, kindlier, or more generous than Leonard's brothers in arms of twenty years ago.

I dare say, even in those brainless times, even among the jovial faces around that mess table, there were some who cared about their profession, had strategic genius, and studied the art of war. At least one did. Everybody challenges the Captain. He was Copleston's guardian. Everybody knows all about him. Then they challenged me, and had I drained all the bumpers they came offering me, my course at that table would have been brief indeed.

"Gentlemen, 'The Queen!'"

It is the President, and then we fall into general talk.

What sort of mess would that be into which Wassielewski was going to introduce me? A mess of peasants sitting round a fire of sticks in a forest. Instead of the Queen's health we should drink to Poland, instead of claret we should have water, instead of a circle of faces in which the enjoyment of life—the mere fact of living—was the prevailing feature, I should see round me everywhere the grim and earnest faces of those who were looking forward sadly to defeat and death. I suppose when a man is going to be martyred he goes to meet his doom with a certain exaltation which enables him to pass through the agony of death with heroic mien. The most disagreeable part about it must be the steady looking forward to the supreme moment.

"Dreamer," whispered Leonard, "where are your thoughts?"

"I was thinking what sort of a regimental mess I should find in Poland," I replied, forgetting that Leonard knew nothing.

"What mess? Poland?" he asked. "What have you to do with Poland now?"

I told him in a few words. It was not the place or the time after dinner at a regimental mess to go into any heroics. Besides, I felt none—only a sad despondency at the necessity which was going to drag into the trouble one who had such small stomach for the fight.

Leonard was aghast.

"The thing is absurd, Laddy, ridiculous. You must not go."

"I have pledged my word," I said, "and I must. You would not have me break old Wassielewski's heart?"

"I don't know. It must be a tough old heart by

this time. But I would rather break that than let him break your head. We will talk about it to-morrow, old boy. What with Celia's troubles and yours, it seems as if we shall have our hands full for awhile. Pray, has the Captain, by accident, got any secret sorrow?"

"No," I replied, laughing. It was beautiful to see the calm way in which Leonard faced difficulties.

"He is not engaged to Mrs. Jeram, I hope, or has not contracted a secret marriage with his cook? He's not going to be tried by court-martial for intoxication, is he? Really, Laddy, you have given me a shock. Are you sure there is no more behind?"

"Quite sure."

"Good. There is going to be a move. We will get away early. I will go and see this fire-eater, and appeal to his common sense."

It was twelve, however, before we escaped the kindly hospitalities of the mess, and the Captain came away amid a storm of invitations to dine with them again. He accepted them all, in great good spirits, and became a sort of privileged person in the barracks so long as that regiment stayed in the place, dividing his time in the afternoon between the officers and the boys at play. When the regiment was ordered away he returned entirely to the boys.

CHAPTER XV.

AN APPEAL TO COMMON SENSE.

"WE will appeal," said Leonard, "to the man's common sense first. The thing is absurd and preposterous."

He did make that appeal to Wassielewski, and as it was a complete failure, I suppose the old conspirator had no common sense.

He called in the morning at his lodgings, that one room which I have described, where the old man told me my own story in all its hideous details, sparing nothing. The Pole was sitting at the table, the map of Poland in his hand, preparing for the campaign. Long lists and estimates lay beside him, with which he was estimating the progress and duration of the struggle. The longer the revolt, the more lives sacrificed, the greater the exasperation and cruelties of the Muscovs, the better for Poland. Tears of women, he used to say in his grim way, and blood of men together fructify the soil, so that it produces heroes.

At sight of a stranger he sprang to his feet, and clutched his papers.

"You do not remember me," said Leonard.

"I do not," replied the old man, gazing keenly and suspiciously into his face. Spies and police assume so many forms that they might even be looked for beneath the guise of a young Englishman. "Who are you, and what do you want with me?"

"My name is Leonard Copleston. I am the old friend of Ladislas Pulaski. One of his only friends."

"He has many," said Wassielewski. "Friends in his own country."

"Friends who will make him the tool of their own purposes, and lead him, if they got their own will, to death. I am one of the friends who want him to live."

Wassielewski made no reply for a moment.

Then he seemed to recollect.

"I know you now," he said. "You went away to seek your fortune. You used to come to our barrack and learn things. The Poles were good to you then."

"Some of your people taught me French and Russian, riding, fencing, all sorts of useful things. I am grateful to them."

"And your fortune—it is found?"

"Yes; I am an officer in the army; I have been in the Crimea."

The old man's face brightened.

"Aha! you fought the Muscovite. We were watching, hoping to fight him too, but our chance never came. Why—why did you not make a demonstration in Poland?"

"We did what we could, and we got the best of it."

The Pole sighed. Then he resumed his suspicious look.

"Why do you come to see me? Can I fiddle for you? I can march before troops of your men playing a hornpipe. What else can I do for you? Ah! I see—I see," his face assumed a look of cunning. "You are a friend of Ladislas Pulaski, and you come here to persuade me not to take him. That is too late. He has pledged himself, and he must keep his word. Say what you have to say, and leave me. I have much to think of."

"What I have to say is short. It is absurd to drag into the meshes of your conspiracy a man like Ladislas, the most peaceful, the most unpractical, the most dreamy of men. Even now, when you half-maddened him with some horrible story of death and torture, his sympathies are only half with you. He cannot speak Polish; he is a quiet English musician, as unfit for a campaign as any girl. Why do you seek to take away his life? What earthly good can his death do to Poland?"

"He is a Pulaski. That is why he must come with us. His father, Roman Pulaski, dragged out ten years of misery in a Siberian mine. Ladislas must strike a blow to revenge him."

"Revenge! revenge!" Leonard cried impatiently.

"Yes, young gentleman," Wassielewski rose to his full height, looking something like an eagle. "Revenge! That is the word. For every cruel and treacherous murder there shall be revenge full and substantial. Did Ladislas tell you the story of his father?"

"No, not yet."

"That is not well. His mother, too, was murdered when the Russians stole her boy, and she ran after the carts through the winter snow, bare-headed, crying and imploring for her child till she could run no longer, and so fell down and died. Did Ladislas tell you of his mother?"

"No."

"It is not well. Ladislas should tell everybody these things. He should repeat them to himself twice a day; he should never let them go out of his brain."

"Why did you disturb the current of his peaceful life with the story?"

"To fire his blood; to quicken his sluggish pulse. The boy is a dreamer. I would spur him into action."

"You cannot do that. But you might spur him into madness. What is the use of filling his thoughts with revenge which can only be dreamed of?"

"Only be dreamed of!" Wassielewski cried, almost with a shriek. "Why, man, I have dreamed of revenge for twenty years and more. Only be dreamed of? Why, we shall put the revenge into action at once. Do you hear?—at once—next week. We start next week—we—but you are an Englishman," he stopped short, "and you would not betray me."

"I betray no one. But Ladislas shall not go with you."

"I say he shall," Wassielewski replied, calmly. "I have persuaded him. He is expected. Revenge? Yes; a long scourge from generation to generation."

"An unworthy thing to seek. I thought you Poles were patriots."

"It is because we are patriots that we seek revenge. How easy it is for you English, who have no wrongs to remember, to talk with contempt of revenge. What do you know of backs scarred and seamed with Russian sticks? What murdered sons have you for the women to lament? What broken promises, ruined homes, outraged hearths, secret wrongs, and brutal imprisonments? Go, sir; leave me alone with my plans ; and talk to no Pole about living in peace."

" He is deformed."

" So much the better. All the Pulaskis for centuries have been tall and straight. Who crippled the boy ? The Russians. Let the people see his round back and hear his story."

" He is weak ; he cannot march ; he cannot even carry a gun."

" Yes ; he is strong enough to carry a rifle, and use it, too."

" He is a dreamer. Let him dream away his life in peace."

" He may dream, if he likes—in the next world," said the conspirator, grimly. " Poland claims all her sons—dreamers, and poets, and all. This is a *levée en masse*, a universal conscription, which knows of no exceptions. He must join the rest, and march to meet his fate. Shall a son of Roman Pulaski stay in inglorious exile while the Poles are rising again ?"

Leonard made a gesture of impatience.

" It is madness. Man, it is murder."

Wassielewski sighed and sat down—he had been

walking up and down the room. Resting one hand upon his papers, he looked up sorrowfully at Leonard, speaking in low tones of conviction and with softened eyes.

"It is what I have said to myself a thousand times. Ladislas is not a soldier: let him live. I say it still, in the day-time. But at night, when I am quite alone in the moonlight, I sometimes see the form of his mother, the Lady Claudia. She is in white, and she points to Poland. Her face is not sad but joyous. Perhaps that is because she is going to have her son again, in Heaven—after the Russians have killed him. I asked her, once, because I wished to save the boy, if he should go. She smiled and pointed her finger still. After that, I knew. She wants to have him with her."

"That was a dream of the night, Wassielewski."

"No—no," he shook his head and laughed; "I am not to be persuaded that it was a dream. Why, I should be mad indeed if I were to take the injunctions of my dear and long-lost mistress to be a dream."

"People are sometimes deceived," said Leonard, "by the very force of their thoughts—by illusions of the brain—by fancies——"

"It seems a cruel thing," Wassielewski went on, unheeding, "but it cannot be cruel, if his mother orders it. The boy must come with me: he must join the villagers: he must learn their language—if he has time: march with them: eat with them: and carry his life in his hand until Death comes for him. It will be bad for him at first, but he will grow stronger, and then he will feel the battle fever, so that when I am killed he will be better able to protect himself. And perhaps he will escape—a good many Poles have escaped. Then you will have him back again. But I do not think he will, because in the night I see visions of battles between the Russians and the Poles, and I never see him among them, even myself."

"Poor Wassielewski," said Leonard, touched with his fanatic simplicity.

"He is a good lad," the old man went on. "I loved him first for his mother's sake, but learned to love him for his own. He has a tender soul, like a woman's, and a face like a girl's. We shall have to accustom him to scenes that he knows nothing of. We do not make war in Poland with kid gloves. We kill and are killed: we shoot and are shot : we use every weapon that we can find and call it lawful. We slaughter every Muscov who falls into our hands, and we expect to be slaughtered ourselves. It is war to the knife between us, and the Poles are always on the losing side."

"Then why make these mad attempts at insurrection ?"

"Because the time has come round again. Once in every generation, sometimes twice, that time comes round. Now it is upon us, and we are ready to move. You wish to save your friend. It is too late ; his name is here, upon the roll of those who dare to die."

"Why," said Leonard, "you are a worse dreamer than poor Ladislas. On whose head will the guilt of all this bloodshed lie, except on yours and the madmen among whom you work ?"

Wassielewski shook his head.

"The crime be on the head of the Czar. Rebellion is my life. I think of it all day, and dream of it all night. By long thinking you come to learn the wishes of the dead. They whisper to me, these voices of the silent night, 'What we died for, you must die for ; what we suffered for, you must suffer for; the soil of Poland is rank with the blood of her martyrs. Do you, too, with the rest, take the musket, and go to lie in that sacred earth.' They have chosen me, the noble dead; they have elected me to join in their fellowship. Ladislas shall sit beside me with them. I have spoken."

He finished, and pointed to the door. There was nothing more to be said, and Leonard came away disheartened.

"It is no use, Ladislas," he said. "The man is mad with long brooding over his wrongs. I have never been much in the conspiracy and rebellion line, but now I understand what a conspirator is like in private life, and I don't like him. When I read henceforth of Guy Fawkes, Damiens, Cassius, Brutus, and other gentlemen of their way of thinking, I shall always remember old Wassielewski, with his deep-set eyes, his overhanging eyebrows, that far-off look of his, and the calm way in which he contemplates being killed. Even Havelock and his saints never marched to death with greater composure. And killed he certainly will be, with all the madmen who go with him."

"I must go with him, Leonard. I have promised. I am pledged."

"We shall see," he replied.

The vague words brought a little hope to my soul. The thirst for revenge, alien to my nature, was gone now, despite the burning wrongs, the shameful and horrible history which the old man had told me. I looked forward with unutterable disgust to a campaign among Polish rebels., I was indeed an unworthy son of Poland.

CHAPTER XVI.

A DIPLOMATIST.

It was not with any view of appealing to Herr Räumer's generosity that Leonard called upon him. Quite the contrary. He went to see what manner of man this alien would appear to him, seen in the light of extended experience. And he avoided all reference to Celia. It was in the forenoon that he went. The German was sitting at his piano playing snatches of sentimental ditties and students' songs with a pipe in his lips, which he occasionally put down to warble something in French or German about Mariette remembering Lindor, and all the rest of it, or "How Love survives Absence," "How Hard it is for Friends to Part." His love for music never carried him beyond the ballad stage, and all the things he played were reminiscences of some time spent among students or young officers at Heidelberg, Vienna, or Paris.

He got up—big, massive, imposing—and greeted his visitor cordially.

"Who comes to see me, drinks with me," he said, hospitably, "always excepting Ladislas Pulaski, who drinks with no one. Sit down, Captain Copleston. I am glad to see you so early. That shows that you are going to talk. So—a cigar—— *Lieb fraumilch*—and good—so. When Fortune means most kindly to a man, she makes him a soldier. I congratulate you."

"You have served yourself?"

"I have—in Austrian cavalry. I had an accident, and could ride no more. That is why I abandoned my career."

"Ah!" said Leonard, thoughtfully, "I knew you had been a soldier. One never quite loses the reminiscences of drill."

They went on talking in idle fashion.

"And you still keep up the same interest in the Poles, Herr Räumer?"

"Poles?" He started. "What interest?"

"When last I saw you, I was learning French at the Polish Barrack, and you used to ask me about them—you remember."

"Ah!—Yes.—So.—Yes. I remember perfectly. The poor Poles. But they are all gone now, except one or two, and I had forgotten them."

"Wassielewski remains. You know him?"

"By name; Ladislas talks about him." This was not true. "He is the irreconcilable Pole—the ideal Pole. A harmless enthusiast."

"Enthusiast, perhaps. Harmless, no."

"There are plenty like him about the world," said the German, quietly. "They seldom do mischief. They are in London, Paris, New York, and Stamboul. They are even in Moscow. Let them conspire."

"No mischief!" Leonard echoed. "The Russians prevent that by their secret service, I suppose." He looked at his friend steadily. "We know by Crimean experience how well that is conducted. Why—they had a Russian spy, disguised as a German, all through the war, in our own London War Office. But that you have heard, of course."

Herr Räumer laughed.

"It was very neatly done. Any other but the English would have foreseen a Russian war, and taken care that some of their officers learned Russian."

"At all events, we get on, somehow."

"Yes; because you have a good geographical position; because you have money; and because you have the most wonderful luck. Wait till Russia gets Stamboul."

"When will that be?"

"And commands the Valley of the Euphrates. It is very clever of you to make of Moldavia and Wallachia an independent state; but who is to guard it? Suppose a time were to come when Austria—she is always Austria the Unready—was fettered with diplomatic chains, when France either would not or could not interfere in the Eastern Question, what is to prevent Russia from marching across the frontier of your Roumania? Treaties? Why, the whole history of the world is the history of broken treaties. Sooner or later she will try for Asia, from the Levant to Pekin. Of course that will include Afghanistan. Then she will try for

India, and win it by force of numbers. Where will your greatness be then?"

"We have fought her before, and we will fight her again."

"Oh yes; you can fight, you English. Perhaps you can fight better than any other people. That is to say, you can do with a hundred soldiers what Russia wants a hundred and twenty to accomplish. But you have only that hundred, and Russia has behind her hundred and twenty ten times a hundred and twenty more. You are commercially great because London has taken the place which the Constantinople of the future will hold, the commercial centre of the world. You have a great fleet. You will lose your great empire because you will not have a great army. England will become less formidable as armies grow greater. If you wish to preserve the power of England, make every Englishman a soldier."

"That will never be," said Leonard.

"Then the days of England's supremacy are done."

He knocked out the ashes of his pipe, refilled it slowly, and lit up again.

"It is by her secret service which you despise that Russia defends herself, and steadily advances. She throws out her secret agents to watch, report, and, if necessary, make mischief. They are the irregular cavalry of politics. Sometimes they are called merchants or scientific explorers, sometimes they are disguised as missionaries, sometimes they are the ministers and rulers of the country, corrupted by Russian gold or flattered with Russian skill. Russia makes no move till she has felt her way. Persia will be hers when the last relic of British influence has been bought out or wheedled out, and when Russian counsels have been able, unmolested, to bring the country into a fit condition for Russian occupation."

"I suppose that Russian influences are already at work in England itself?"

"Not yet," said Herr Räumer, laughing. "The conquest of England would cost too much. But Russian influences are already at work against British interests, wherever they can be met and injured. You have no enemy in the world except Russia. Not France, which changes her policy as she changes her Government, once in every generation. Not America, which is a peaceful country, and more afraid of war than England. The enemy of England, the persistent and ever watchful enemy of England, is Russia, because it is England alone, at present, that can keep Russia from Constantinople."

"Well, you have forewarned us, at all events."

"Forewarned is nothing. You may forewarn a consumptive man that he will suffer in the lungs. That will not prevent the disease. You will go on in England, as you always do, learning nothing, preparing for nothing, acting always as if you had to do with men who tell the truth. Could any country be more stupid?"

"Why," asked Leonard, "should not nations be as honest as men?"

"So they are," he replied, "only you Englishmen will persist in supposing that men are not liars. An English gentleman, I will admit, always speaks the truth. At least, he has been taught to do so, and it comes natural to him. But a common Englishman does not. The man who sells things to you lies habitually, in order to make his profit—lies like a Syrian, goes to church on Sundays, and thinks he is a Christian. An American, I suppose, is pretty nearly the same thing as an Englishman, unless he happens to be an Irish Catholic. I believe that Dutchmen, Danes, Swedes, and Norwegians—small nations without ambition—have a singular preference for the truth. But all other nations lie. I am a German, and I state that unblushingly. Those get on best who lie hardest."

"Suppose that one here and there were to speak the truth?"

"It would do him no good, because he would not be believed, unless he were an Englishman. Diplomacy is a game in which no one believes any one else. The truth lies behind the words—somewhere. It is our business—I mean the business of diplomatists—to find it out. First, you have the actual assurance of the Czar, we will say, conveyed by his ambassador. Of course no one, except, perhaps, an English newspaper, pretends for a moment to believe a pacific assurance. You receive it, and you try to find out what Russia is actually doing, which is a great deal more important. If you find that out, and are able to watch the movements of other Powers, you have a chance of understanding the truth.

"Everything stated openly is stated with intention to deceive. That is the first rule in diplomacy. All friendly assurances must be received with suspicion. That is the second rule. The statement of disinterested action which is always made is, of course, received with derision. No nation is disinterested, except, sometimes, England. There has not been a disinterested action done by any single nation since the world began, save only one or two done by England. I grant you that. Statesmanship means lying for the good of your country, and there is a regular method which is known and adopted everywhere. Except to the ignorant people, it means nothing, and imposes on no one."

"Why not start fair again all round, and speak the truth?"

"What? and spoil the game? Heaven forbid! We have our little fictions in society, why not in diplomacy also? I do not want, as I once told Ladislas Pulaski, to live in a world gone good. It would be tedious to me, that kind of world. And, at my age, I cannot unlearn things. Let us go on as we have always gone on—one nation trying to cheat every other—ambassadors lying—secret service reduced to one of the fine arts—and let us watch the splendid spectacle, unequalled in history, of a nation following a line of policy from generation to generation, beaten at one point and carrying it forward at another—always advancing, always aided everywhere by a swarm of secret agents."

Afterwards repeating the conversation to me,—

"The man," said Leonard, "is a Russian agent himself. I am certain of it. No German ever talked English so well: he has the best Russian manner: he is *rusé*, polished, and utterly cynically frank, unscrupulous, like all the people connected with the Russian Government. He has an important mission here, no doubt, and must have picked up a good deal of information during all these years. I wonder what his name is, and what his real rank in the police."

"You are only guessing, Leonard."

"Perhaps, but I am sure, all the same. My dear boy, I know them. There were Russian papers on the table, too. I saw the *Golos*, of Moscow, among others. He is no more a German than you or I. 'Served in the Austrian cavalry.' Fudge and flap-doodle! as Mrs. Pontifex says. Curious, to see the patronising way in which he talked. I am only a young officer of that stupid nation where diplomatists speak the truth. I should like to checkmate our friend on his own ground."

"But—Celia?"

"Do you think I am going to let Celia be handed over to a Russian spy?" he asked, grandly. "A Russian officer would be a different thing. There are splendid fellows among them. But a spy? Pah! The thought makes me feel ill. Besides, Laddy," he laughed, "I don't think we will let Celia go out of England at all. She is too good for any but an Englishman."

CHAPTER XVII.

THE FOURTH ESTATE.

I WAS sitting in Leonard's quarters two days afterwards, idling the time with him, when I became aware of a familiar figure walking slowly across the barrack yard. It was that of Mr. Ferdinand Brambler. I had not seen any of the family for some time, having been entirely occupied with Celia, Leonard, and my Polish schemes. He bore himself with quite his old solemnity, but there was something in his manner which showed change and decay—a kind of mouldiness. As he drew nearer it became too evident that his outer garments were much the worse for wear, his boots down at heel, and his whole appearance pinched and hungry. Things must have been going badly with the children. My heart smote me for neglecting the Bramblers. Were all of them, including my poor little bright-eyed Forty-four, in the same hungry and dilapidated condition ?

He made straight for Leonard's quarters, and, coming in out of the broad sunlight, did not at first see me.

" Captain Copleston ?" he asked timidly.

" I am Captain Copleston," said Leonard. " What can I do for you ?"

" Sir," said the great Ferdinand, drawing himself up, " I introduce myself as representing the Fourth Estate. I am the Printing Press."

" You don't look like one," replied Leonard flippantly. " But go on."

" Don't you know me, Mr. Ferdinand ?" I asked, jumping up and shaking hands with him. " Leonard, this is my old friend, Mr. Ferdinand Brambler, the brother of Augustus Brambler, whom you recollect, I am sure."

" Of course I do," said Leonard. " How do you do, Mr. Brambler ? Your brother was a little man, with a comical face that looked as if he was too jolly for his work. I remember now. Is he in the

Legal now, in the Clerical, or in the Scholastic? And will you take a glass of wine or a brandy and soda?"

"My brother Augustus devotes his whole energies now to the Legal," said Ferdinand, slowly. "I will take a brandy and soda, thank you. With a biscuit or a sandwich, if I may ask for one."

"Send for some sandwiches, Leonard," I said. "And how are you all in Castle Street?"

"But poorly, Mr. Pulaski. Very poorly. The children are—not to disguise the truth—ahem—breaking out again, in a way dreadful to look at. Forty-six is nothing but an Object—an Object—from insufficiency of diet. Too much bread and too little meat. Ah! the good old days are gone when things were going on—things worthy of an historic pen—all round us, and money flowed in—literally flowed in, Captain Copleston. What with a prize ship here, an embarkation of troops there, the return of the wounded, an inspection of militia, and all the launches, I used to think nothing of writing up to a leg of mutton in three or four hours, turning off a pair of boots as if it was nothing, putting a greatcoat into shape in a single evening, throwing in a gown for Mrs. Augustus and a new frock for Forty-four, or going out in the morning, and polishing off a day's run into the country for the whole family out of a visit from the Commander-in-Chief. I used to laugh at that as only a good day's work. Happy time! You remember how fat and well-fed the children were once, Mr. Pulaski. But those days are gone. I despised then what I used to call the butter and eggs. Alas! the butter and eggs are nearly all we have to live upon now."

"You mean——"

"I mean, gentlemen, the short paragraphs poorly remunerated at one penny for each line of copy. One penny! And at least half of the sum goes in wear and tear of shoe leather worn out in picking up items about the town. I am a *chiffonier*, gentlemen, as we say in the French. I pick up rags and tatters of information as I peregrinate the streets. Nothing is too trifling for my degraded pen. I find myself even, in the children's interests, praying for a fire or a murder, or a neat case of robbery. Here, for instance, is a specimen of how low in the literary scale we can go."

He pulled a little bundle of papers out of his pocket.

"'SINGULAR ACCIDENT.

"'As our esteemed townsman, Alderman Cherrystone, was walking along the pavement of High Street on the morning of Monday last, he stepped upon a piece of orange peel, and falling heavily, dislocated his arm. The unfortunate gentleman, who has been removed to the hospital, is now doing well.'

"Mr. Pulaski," he asked in withering sarcasm, "that is a pleasant thing to come to after all my grandeur, is it not? Think of it, you who actually remember my papers on the arrival and departure of troops. But it is sixpence," he added with a sigh. "Here is another of the same sort. I call it," he added in a sepulchral voice,

"'A LIKELY STORY.

"'On Thursday, before His Worship the Mayor, a young man of dissipated appearance, who gave the name of Moses Copleston——'"

"What?" cried Leonard, "Moses Copleston?"

"Yes, sir, your own name was that given by that individual."

"Go on," said Lonard, looking at me.

"'And said he was the son of a general in the army, was charged with being drunk and disorderly in the streets. The police knew him well, and various committals made in another name were reported of him. He was fined 40s. and costs, or a fortnight. The money was instantly paid, and the prisoner left the Court laughing, and saying there was plenty more to be got where that came from.'"

"'The Mayor recalled him——'"

"Will you give me that paragraph?" Leonard interrupted, and with an excited air. "Will you allow me to keep that out of the paper? I have a reason—it is my own name, you see."

"Certainly, sir," said Ferdinand. "I have no wish to put it into the paper, except that it is worth fourteenpence. And that goes some way towards the children's dinner, poor things."

"I will give you more than fourteenpence for it, my good friend," said Leonard. "Where is this prisoner—this Moses—do you know?"

Of course I perceived the suspicion that had entered his mind. He was jumping at conclusions, as usual, but it was hard not to believe that he was right. I began to think what we knew of our old enemy Moses, and could remember nothing except what Jem Hex—Boatswain Hex—told me—that he was not a credit to his education. This was but a small clue. But some shots in the dark go straight to the bull's eye. Leonard's eye met mine, and there was certainty in it.

I saw he wanted to talk about it, and so I got rid of Ferdinand by proposing to bring Leonard to his house in the evening, when he should pump him, and extract materials for a dozen papers.

"It is very kind of you, sir," he said. "You will enable me to confer on the children next week—ahem—a sense of repletion that they have not experienced for many months."

"I will tell you anything you want," said Leonard. "But you must ask me, because I cannot know, beforehand, what you would most like to have."

"Sir," said Ferdinand fervently, "I will pump you to good purpose if you will allow me. Your own exploits, ahem——"

"No—no," said Leonard, laughing. "I must

make conditions. You must keep my name out of your story."

Ferdinand's countenance fell.

"If you insist upon it—of course. But personalities are the soul of successful journalism"—it will be seen that Ferdinand Brambler was in advance of his age—"and if I *could* be permitted to describe these modest quarters in detail—camp-bed. two chairs, absence of ornament—ah!—'The Hero's Retreat;' your personal appearance, tall, with curling brown hair, square shoulders, manly and assured carriage, eagle eye—ah!—'The Hero at Home;' your conversation—'with difficulty can he be induced to speak of those hairbreadth escapes, those feats of more than British pluck, those audacious sorties'—'The Hero in Modesty;' your dress when not on duty, a plain suit of tweed, without personal decoration of any kind, simple, severe, and in good taste—'The Hero in Mufti;' and your early life, a native of this town, educated partly by Mr. Hezekiah Ryler, B.A., at the time when Mr. Augustus Brambler formed part of his competent and efficient staff, and partly by the learned Perpetual Curate of St. Faith's—'The Hero's Education;'

your entrance into the army, 'The Hero takes his First Step——'"

"Stop—stop—for Heaven's sake," cried the Hero. "Do you believe I am going to consent to that kind of thing?"

Ferdinand collapsed.

"If you really will not allow it," he said, "there is nothing more to be done. Just as I was warming into the subject, too. Well, Captain Copleston, if you will not let me describe your own exploits by name, I shall be grateful for any particulars you may be kind enough to give me."

"Yes—on those conditions, that my name is kept out—I shall be glad to help you."

"Sir," said Ferdinand, "you are very good. I will pump you like—like—an organ-blower. I will play on you like—like a Handel. At what time, sir, will you honour our humble abode?"

"We will be with you about eight," I said. "And—and—Mrs. Ferdinand, will you give my compliments to Mrs. Augustus, and my love to Forty-four, and say that we hope to have the pleasure of supper with them. Early supper, so as to suit Forty-six and the rest."

Ferdinand sighed, and then smiled, and then with a deep bow to the Hero, retired.

"What about Moses?" cried Leonard.

"How do you know it is the real Moses?"

"There can be but one Moses," said Leonard; "and how should any other get hold of my name? Do you think he is in the town now?"

I began to make inquiries that very afternoon, bethinking me that Mrs. Hex, Jem the Bo's'n's wife, might know something about it. Jem had been married some time now, and was the father of a young family, who lived in one of the streets near Victory Row in a highly respectable manner. Mrs. Hex had been a young lady connected on both sides with the service, so that it was quite natural that she should marry a sailor, and it was an advantageous match on both sides. She remembered Moses perfectly well; he was always going and coming, she said; would be seen about for a day or two, and would then disappear for a long time; he had been in prison once for something or other; then he disappeared for some years; then he came back in rags; and then—just a short time ago—he suddenly blossomed out into new and magnificent toggery, with a gold watch-chain and a real watch, with rings on his fingers, and money in his pocket, and he got drunk every night. Also, he called himself Copleston, which Mrs. Hex thought should not be allowed. Most likely we might find him at the Blue Anchor in the evening, where there was a nightly free-and-easy for soldiers and sailors, at which he often appeared, standing drinks all round in a free and affable manner.

"Quite the Moses we used to love," said Leonard in a great rage. "We will go to the Blue Anchor and wring the truth out of him."

For that day we had, however, our engagement at the Bramblers', which we duly kept, and were ushered into the front room, Ferdinand's "study." He was sitting at the table in expectation of us, with paper and pencil before him. He was hungering and thirsting for information. Beside him stood Augustus, as cheerful and smiling as though the children were not breaking out. Except that he was shabbier than usual, there was no mark of poverty or failure upon him.

"This, Captain Copleston," he said, "is a real honour. I take it as a recognition of my brother

Ferdinand's genius. My brother Ferdinand, sir, is a Gem."

"Brother Augustus," murmured the author bashfully, "nay—nay."

"A Gem—I repeat it—a Gem. And of the first water. What says the poet?—

> "Full many a time, this Gem of ray serene,
> Outside the *Journal* Office may be seen.'

He will do you justice, sir. Mr. Pulaski," he sank his voice to a whisper, "shall we leave these two alone? Shall we retire to the domestic circle, not to disturb History and Heroism? At what time shall we name supper, Captain Copleston? Pray, fix your own time. Think of your convenience first. We are nothing—nothing."

"I never take supper, thank you," said Leonard, who was beginning to be a little bored with the whole business.

"Don't speak of supper to me," said Ferdinand. "This is my supper," he patted the paper affectionately. "This my evening beer." He pointed to the inkstand. "This is my pillow," indicating the blotting-pad. "And for me there will be no night's rest. Now, sir, if you will sit there—so—with the light upon your face—we can converse. Affluence is about to return, brother Augustus."

Augustus and I stole out of the room on tiptoe. In the back room the table was laid, and the children were crowded in the window, looking at the cloth with longing eyes. Poor little children! They were grown pale and thin during these hard times, and their clothes were desperately shabby. Forty-four, a tall girl now of fourteen, angular and bony, as is common at that age, preserved some show of cheerfulness, as became the eldest of the family. It was hers to set an example. But the rest were very sad in countenance, save for a sort of hungry joy raised by the prospect of supper.

"Always something kind from the Captain," murmured the poor wife.

"It *was* lucky," I said, "that we had that cold round of beef in the larder. Cannot we have supper immediately? I am sure the children would like it."

The poor children gave a cry, and Forty-six burst into loud weeping.

"Things have not gone very well, latterly," said Augustus, looking uncomfortable. "Sometimes I even think that we don't get enough meat. We had some on Sunday, I remember"—and this was Friday—"because Ferdinand said it was the first real meal he had enjoyed for a week. That was while we were sitting over our wine after dinner."

Nothing, not even actual starvation, would have prevented the two brothers from enjoying their Sunday pretence of sitting, one each side a little table, at the front window, with a decanter and two glasses before them. I do not know what the decanter contained. Perhaps what had once been Marsala. Ferdinand cherished the custom as a mark of true gentility, and was exceedingly angry if the children came in and interrupted. He said grandly that a gentleman "ought not to be disturbed over his wine." I think Augustus cared less about the ceremony.

Meantime the mother, assisted by Forty-four and Forty-five, brought in the supper—cold beef and hot potatoes—with real beer—no toast and water.

I pass over the details of the meal. Even Augustus was too hungry to talk, and Forty-six surpassed himself. I sat next to Forty-four, who squeezed my hand furtively, to show that she was grateful to the Captain. She was always a tender-hearted little thing, and devoted to her brothers and sisters. The pangs of hunger appeased, we talked.

"You have now an opportunity," said Augustus, leaning back in his chair after the fatigues of eating; "you have now an opportunity of boasting, my children, that a Crimean hero has actually come to this house, in order to tell the history of the war to your uncle Ferdinand, the well-known writer."

The boys and girls murmured. This was indeed grandeur.

"We will drink," said Augustus, filling his glass, and handing me the jug. "We will drink a toast. I give you, children, coupled, the names of Captain Copleston, the Hero, and Ferdinand Brambler (your uncle, my dears), the historian. It is my firm belief that this night has commenced what I may in military language call an Alliance, or—speaking as a lawyer, one may say that this night has witnessed the tacit execution of a Deed of Partnership—a Deed of Partnership"—he relished his words so much that he was fain to repeat them

—"between the Hero and the Historian, which will result in their being known together, and indissolubly connected by the generations, yet to come, of posterity. For myself, I have, as you know, little other ambition than to be remembered, if remembered I am at all, as Augustus Brambler (your father, my dears), formerly an ornament to the Legal."

We drank the toast with enthusiasm. There were nowhere to be found children more ready to drink or eat toasts than the Bramblers.

"By our own family connections, Mr. Pulaski," Augustus continued, "we have more sympathy with the Navy than with the Army. Mrs. Brambler —your mother, my dears—is highly connected as regards that service; and it is, I confess, my favourite. Sometimes I think of putting Forty-six into it, though if they were wrecked on a desert island, and provisions ran short, he would come off badly. Forty-eight, of course, is out of the question where discipline and obedience are concerned. It would, however, have been just the service for poor little Fifty-one, my dears, had that interesting child been born."

He looked critically at Forty-six, sadly at Forty-eight, and shook his head. All hung their heads sorrowfully, as was customary at mention of the Great and Gifted Fifty-one—unborn.

"Two members of my wife's family—she was a Tollerwinch—were members of that gallant service, Mr. Pulaski. One of them, her uncle, held the rank of Master's Mate, and, if he had not had the misfortune to knock down his superior officer on the quarter-deck, would now, one may be justified in supposing, have been Rear-Admiral Sir Samuel Tollerwinch, K.C.B.—of the White. I drink to the health and memory—in solemn silence—of the late Admiral."

Such was Augustus's enthusiasm, that we all believed at the moment the deceased officer to have died in that rank.

"The Admiral," Augustus sighed. "You must not be proud, my dears, of these accidents—mere accidents—of distinguished family connections. Your mother's first cousin, James Elderberry, entered the service also. He was a purser's clerk. I think I am right, my dear, in stating to Mr. Pulaski that James was a most gallant and deserving officer."

"He was, indeed," said Mrs. Brambler. "Poor Jem! And sang a most beautiful song when sober."

"Universally esteemed, my children, from the yardarm—to speak nautically—and the maintop mizenmast, wherever that or any other portion of the rigging is lashed taut to the shrouds, down to the orlop deck. His service was not long—only three weeks in all—and it was cut short by a court-martial on a charge of—of—in fact, of inebriation while on duty. He might have done well, perhaps. in some other Walk—or shall we say, Sail of Life? —if he had not, in fact, continued so. He succumbed—remember this, Forty-six—to the effects of thirst. Well, we must all die. To every brave rover comes his day." Augustus rolled his head and tried to look like a buccaneer. "Your mother's cousin, my children, must be regarded as one who fell—in action."

END OF VOL. II.

www.ingramcontent.com/pod-product-compliance
Lightning Source LLC
Chambersburg PA
CBHW031343070726
47496CB00017B/1633
* 9 7 8 3 3 3 7 0 7 9 0 7 9 *